PARADOX 2

Beyond Eternity

PHILLIP P. PETERSON

Translated by
LAURA RADOSH

Edited by
JENNY PIENING

Chapter 1

I'm dead.

But I'm here!

I'm not dead?

David felt like he was falling; he was having trouble thinking clearly. As if he'd been drugged, or was in a delirium. Like that time he'd been brought to the hospital with an infection. It had taken him forever to figure out where he was after waking up.

His eyes were still closed, he realized. A dull throbbing spread from somewhere behind his brow to the rest of his head. And he wasn't falling after all; he was lying on a soft surface. Also like back in the hospital. He could feel the blood beating in his arteries, but otherwise it was quiet. He groaned, and the sound of his own voice echoed in his ears.

He had to open his eyes, find out where he was. But it was a herculean task. His eyelids seemed to be made out of cement. Or maybe he didn't have any? After all, he *was* dead.

But how had he died? He tried to remember, unsuccessfully. Disconnected and muddled fragments of memories entered his consciousness, and vanished again in a sea of agony.

Sudden panic flooded his body with adrenaline. Terrified, he tore his eyes open. Bright. Too bright. The pounding in his head intensified until it felt like he was being beaten by a hammer. He closed his eyes again in torment. At least now he was sure that he had eyes. And therefore also a body. Which meant he could not be dead. But where *was* he?

He opened his eyelids again, slowly and cautiously this time. It was still too bright. Tears formed and blurred his vision. He blinked. There was a white surface in front of him. He blinked again. The white surface was a ceiling. David tried to raise his right arm, but it cost him a colossal effort. He made a fist with his right hand and noticed that he was holding onto something soft. It felt like ... like ... like what? Something familiar, but he was still woozy, it was impossible to concentrate.

Carefully, he turned his head, leaving his eyes open. The ceiling gave way to a wall covered in polychrome dots. He blinked again. Slowly, the image came into focus. The spots turned out to be pictures hanging on a wall, and shelves holding thick books. Again, everything seemed familiar. Then his eyes lit upon a gray stuffed elephant wearing a blue polka-dot scarf, sitting on a wooden chair with a friendly smile.

David finally realized where he was and chuckled inwardly.

I'm home!

Reassured, he closed his eyes again. The familiar environment instilled an almost uncanny confidence.

I'm home! Everything's alright.

There was only one place in the world that he'd ever

felt so at ease. It was the only place he had always, without a second's hesitation, called "home": his old room in his parent's house.

But why did he feel so dazed? And what was wrong with his memory? He couldn't even concentrate! Had he been sick, and his parents had brought him to their place? David tried desperately to remember the last thing that had happened before he'd fallen asleep, but it wouldn't come to him. He must have left work to visit his parents in Athens, and then fallen ill. Had he eaten something rotten and contracted food poisoning?

He opened his eyes again. The light hurt a little bit less. It wasn't that bright after all. The sun was definitely not shining; if it were, it would have cast the shadow of the window frame on the wall in front of him. Everything looked just the way he remembered. There were the posters of Nirvana and Pearl Jam, who he'd been into for a while as a teenager. Next to them hung that photo of Albert Einstein sticking out his tongue. There were five tomes on the shelf that his father had hung somewhat crookedly. One book about physics, one on mathematics, two programming manuals for C++ and Java, and a complete guide to all *Star Trek* episodes. Next to the shelf hung a gray analog clock. It was almost nine thirty.

David turned his head a bit further to take in his old desk next to the window. It was more suited to a schoolkid than an adult doctoral candidate, and had been the cause of much back pain during semester breaks. A silver lamp stood on the desk, and "e=2.718281" was scrawled in pencil on the wallpaper above it.

It was very quiet. Usually you could hear cars driving past the house on their way into the city. Was today maybe a holiday?

David jumped when he heard somebody clear their

3

throat at his other side. It was a sound he knew from earliest childhood. His father used to come into his room in the morning when it was time for him to get up. Those days were long gone, but the sound had been etched into David's memory.

"Hi, Dad!"

David was horrified. Was that hoarse rasp really his own voice? Sluggishly, as if in slow motion, he turned his head.

And there was his father, sitting next to his old wooden wardrobe. He was leaning back comfortably in the old brown leather recliner to which David had always retreated to indulge in science fiction novels. His father flashed a quick smile and looked at him lovingly through his frame-less glasses. His old man had a professorly look about him, maybe because he was a lecturer at the history department of the local community college. Now his advancing age, gray hair, and neatly trimmed beard, together with the light gray jacket that he wore indoors even in the summer, did the rest to create a kind of elder statesman image— always ready with good advice or an intelligent question, but never pushy.

"How long have you been sitting there?" David asked. He really was hoarse. He coughed and noticed that his throat was completely dry. He reached for the bedside table, where a small bottle of still water stood as always. He unscrewed the cap with trembling hands and drank greedily. The water was surprisingly cool.

"Quite a while," his father answered gently.

David put the bottle back on the table. Slowly, he propped himself up in bed—to which his head reacted by throbbing even more. He coughed again.

"What happened?"

"You screamed in your sleep," his father answered.

"Am I sick?"

His father slowly cocked his head. "How do you feel?"

"Awful. A little bit like the time I had that fever."

"So you remember that?"

David nodded weakly.

"What else do you remember?" his father asked. His voice was strangely devoid of emotion. Like he was asking the question even though he didn't really care about the answer. As if he were thinking about something else. But he looked at David with interest.

"I don't know. I think I had a blackout. My last coherent memory is a morning at work at Centauri. After that, it's just fragments. I don't even remember flying here."

"And you don't remember anything else?"

"Should I?" David replied

His father smiled at him. "You tell me."

David closed his eyes. He felt a little less woozy. But he was still having trouble concentrating. When he closed his eyes, he felt again like he was falling. Or like he was weightless.

Weightless?

Hazy images swiftly superimposed themselves upon his inner eye. The inside of a spaceship. Earth from orbit. The moon gliding slowly past him.

"I must have been dreaming," David said, looking at his father. "A very realistic dream."

"What did you dream, David?" his father asked, again without the slightest emotion.

"I can't really say. I think I was in space. On a spaceship. On a Centauri mission."

"Was it a good dream?"

David had trouble answering and tried to recall his feelings. At first, the dream had been good. He had felt adventurous. And then there was the liberating sense of floating, and the knowledge that he was part of something special and about to make new discoveries. "In the beginning, yes," he said slowly. "But in the end it was horrible. Threatening. I was locked up and felt hopelessness, then panic. I was scared to death, in fact. Like I was suffocating. I really thought I was dead."

"But now you're awake," his father said. David realized that he hadn't changed his position in the chair the whole time.

"Yes," he answered, and nodded. "Now I'm awake." He grabbed a corner of the bedcovers and pushed them aside. He was wearing only a white T-shirt and white underwear. Groaning, he swung his legs over to sit on the edge of the mattress. His feet dangled a few inches above the floor.

"Are you sure you want to get up already?" his father asked.

David only nodded in answer. Probably it would be best to just lie back down, close his eyes, and allow himself a couple more hours of sleep. But he felt compelled to get back on his feet quickly. That dream… More and more images were coming back to him. And unlike most dreams, which slowly fade from memory after waking up, this one became clearer and clearer the more David thought about it. He saw a face, staring at him accusingly. A man of about fifty dressed in blue astronaut overalls, a helmet under his arm.

"Ed," David whispered. But where did he know the guy from? Had it really been a dream?

"What are you thinking about, David?" his father asked.

"I can't stop thinking about the dream. It was so realistic. I was on an expedition to the edge of our solar system. In the end, everything went wrong and I died."

"What went wrong?"

David looked at his father for a second, then blinked his eyes rapidly. "I don't remember."

His heartbeat began to accelerate and he suddenly felt like he was still dreaming. He looked to the left where the window was, and at the flowing white curtains that cut out the outside world. He had the strange feeling that behind them he would only see the endless white void of the afterworld. The unsettling feeling became stronger and stronger.

He held onto the nightstand to steady himself and slid slowly from the mattress.

"I wouldn't do that if I were you," his father said.

David got goose bumps at the sound of the robotic voice.

What's behind the curtains?

Finally, David was on his own two feet. Leadenly, he stood upright. With heavy steps, he approached the window. He reached slowly for the curtains with his right hand, holding on to the wardrobe for balance with his left. He turned his head toward his father, who still sat immobile in the recliner. "Why not? What's out there?" he asked, his voice trembling.

The old man just smiled.

Panic gripped David's chest. This was not his home. Wherever he was, it was somewhere completely different. A sinister place, where he was being held prisoner. As soon as he pulled back the curtains, he would learn the truth.

He summoned all his courage, jerked the fabric to the side, and exhaled audibly.

Everything was as it should be. The street below. The house across the street, its white facade worn to a stained, peeling yellow due to Mr. Dingle's laziness. The tree a bit to the left, where the crows always roosted in the winter.

"It's just you still seem pretty weak," his father finally said. "I wouldn't want you to fall."

David nodded, relieved, and turned his gaze away from the outside world. But he stayed at the window, steadying himself on the wardrobe.

"I still don't remember how I got here from Portland."

"You slept a long time."

"That doesn't answer my question."

"You didn't ask a question." His father smiled again.

"Yes I did. I said I have no idea how I got here."

"That's a statement, not a question."

David rolled his eyes. *Typical Dad.*

"OK. How long have I been here?"

"About two days. Most of that time you were sleeping."

David nodded. Maybe he was just overworked and had collapsed. The workload at Centauri was crazy. Usually he brought work home and sat at his desk until late in the night. The last time he'd visited his parents he'd also spent the whole first day in bed. It must have been really bad this time. He should really make sure to take it a little easier in the future.

"Is Mom home?" he asked.

His father shook his head. "She's not here."

"Where is she?"

"She's not here."

Maybe it was a Sunday and she was at church. After which she usually went for coffee at the O'Hara's with Aunt Ruth and Uncle Herman. How late was it again? David looked at the clock and started. Hadn't it just been almost nine thirty? That must have been a few minutes ago, but the clock still told the same time.

"The clock's stopped," he said. For some reason, it bothered him more than it should.

"Time is unimportant," his father replied.

Again, David broke out in goose bumps. The whole situation was just so ... weird. He couldn't shake the feeling that he wasn't supposed to be here.

David pushed the curtains back a little bit further. It was quiet outside. Way too quiet—even for a holiday. Not a single car had driven by the entire time. And he couldn't see any pedestrians, either. No sound of traffic from the nearby highway, no dogs barking—nothing. His gaze wandered skywards. There were only a few cumulus clouds floating above the houses.

Wait a second.

The clouds weren't moving. They stood in the sky like they'd been painted on a blue canvas. The whole environment outside the window was dead. Like a screen, a simulation.

Simulation?

As if someone had turned on a switch in David's head, images flooded in. The space mission dream became even more real. Frighteningly real. He could even remember the names of the three astronauts on his crew: Ed, Grace, and Wendy. They'd been together on a spaceship—what was it called again? They'd flown to the edge of the solar system and suddenly all the stars were gone. Instead they'd met a sentience, eons old, that had surrounded all planetary systems of the galaxy with Dyson spheres, and simulated the starry sky for humanity.

Simulation!

Slowly he turned and stared at the man sitting in the chair, looking for all the world like his father. The man returned his gaze with a friendly smile.

"You're not my father," David stated. "Right?"

The stranger nodded. "Right."

"You're just a simulation. Or more like an illusion."

"That is correct."

"And this is not my room."

"Also correct."

David turned his head away. The clouds still hadn't moved an inch across the sky. "And I'm not on Earth at all."

"It is good that you remember."

Slowly David approached the man who was so much like his father. The smile ... the slightly mocking expression in his eyes ...

He stopped in front of the chair and squatted until he was staring the doppelgänger squarely in the face. The man blinked once and stared into David's eyes.

David reached out his hand. He hesitated for a moment and then touched the alien creature's cheek. He had expected to feel nothing beneath his fingers, like when you try to touch a hologram, but his skin was warm and soft, as if he were a flesh-and-blood person.

"Why the illusion?" David asked.

"The familiar environment was created to make waking up easier for you."

Now, David's final memories returned. They'd used the antimatter stores of the Helios—that was the name—to create a hole in the shield around the galaxy, in order to make contact with Earth. Their plan had worked. He himself had pushed the button that sent the message. Then Ed had fallen into the antimatter exhaust and died. In the end, alien nanomachines had begun destroying their space-ship. There had been a tear in the skin of the cockpit, and the last thing he remembered was the feeling of suffocating as the ship's oxygen dissipated into the vacuum of space. But obviously the artificial intelligence had saved them

after all. Or at least saved him. So he must still be somewhere at the sphere. Out there in the outer reaches of the
solar system.

"Where exactly am I?"

"Inside an asteroid, which we have prepared for you
and your companions."

His heart jumped a beat. "Wendy and Grace are
alive too?"

"Yes." The man who looked like his father nodded.

David stood up and took a step back. His legs trembled
and he sat back down on the bed before he lost his balance.
"Where are they? Can I see them?"

"If that is your desire, I can bring you to them. Do you
feel strong enough? Are you thirsty? Hungry?"

Now that he mentioned it, David did notice his
stomach felt pretty empty. He must not have eaten for a
while. His thirst he had pretty much stilled with the bottle
of water from the nightstand.

"Yeah, I am hungry," he admitted.

His father's doppelgänger stood up from the recliner.
"Wait a minute. I'll bring you breakfast."

Breakfast ...

David just nodded.

"You'll find something to wear in the wardrobe. I'll be
right back."

The doppelgänger headed straight for the door. He
actually had his father's slightly skittish gait. When he
opened the door, the light behind it was so bright, it was
impossible for David to make out what lay beyond the
room. He was willing to bet that it looked nothing like the
hallway of his parents' house in Athens.

Inside an asteroid ... There were more than enough of
those in the outer solar system. And some of them were
pretty large. The artificial intelligence must have quickly

hollowed it out and provided an atmosphere, and then set it up to look like this. Or maybe the room had been here for a while and Q—the name they'd given to the alien intelligence—had had the foresight to fix it up for first contact with human beings. How much time had passed since Ed's death and the destruction of the Helios? Hours? Days? Maybe even weeks? David did not have the slightest idea.

He stood up and took two steps to the solid oak wardrobe. Almost falling, he caught himself on the door. He took a few deep breaths and then opened it.

In his real room, the wardrobe was always stuffed to the gills with old shirts he had never thrown away because he planned to give them to Goodwill one day. Next to them hung jackets he never wore and masses of T-shirts, sweatshirts, underwear, and socks flung haphazardly into the shelves.

This wardrobe was bare. David opened the second door, but behind it was the same emptiness. Only one shelf, usually full of gloves and scarves for the winter, held a blue outfit. He pulled it out and immediately recognized the Helios expedition logo. It was the regulation clothing they all had worn aboard the spaceship. Except it couldn't have been from the Helios, because the clothes he'd had with him had signs of wear and tear, while these were brand-new. They even had a new, synthetic smell. Probably they were replicas.

Carefully, David stepped into the pants. It took great concentration not to fall down. Then he pulled on the jacket and closed the zipper. It fit him better than the original.

At the same moment, his father's doppelgänger entered the room. In one hand he was balancing a tray, with the other he closed the door behind him. He walked around the bed and put the food on the nightstand before sitting back down in the chair.

"Thank you," David said, and bent over the gray plastic tray, which could have been from any cafeteria. A sandwich sat on a china plate. Next to the plate was a glass. David picked it up and sniffed.

"Is this real orange juice?" he asked skeptically.

The stranger nodded. "Yes, it is."

"Pressed from real oranges?"

"No, that is not the case."

David looked up in irritation, and then shrugged. Must be some synthetic product. But probably at the molecular level it couldn't be distinguished from real orange juice. He took a sip, the cool liquid really tasted fresh squeezed. He even got pulp between his teeth. Putting the glass down again, David reached for the sandwich. He pulled apart the slices of white bread. Peanut butter! He began to laugh.

"What's so funny?" the doppelgänger asked.

"You," David answered. "You're so funny. My father always made me peanut-butter sandwiches when I was home sick and Mom wasn't there. Is there anything you don't know about me?"

"In fact, no." The stranger with his father's face continued to smile.

"Why did you destroy the Helios?"

"The presence of your ship outside the sphere had not been approved. The damage to the membrane was categorized as an attack. The destruction of your spaceship was the logical consequence."

"But you saved me, Wendy, and Grace," David contested.

"That is correct."

"Why didn't you just let us die?"

"Life in the universe is infinitely precious. We would never destroy it without good reason."

"But we were able to send a message to Earth. We won. Why not just let us fly back?"

The stranger laughed quietly. Just like his father always had whenever David had said or done something amusing as a child. "I'm afraid I must disappoint you. Earth did not receive your message. Nevertheless, we had to prevent you from committing any more acts of sabotage."

"That's why you destroyed the Helios," David concluded. "And that's why you brought us into this asteroid. I guess this will be our prison for the rest of our lives."

The doppelgänger shook his head. "No. That is not the plan."

"And what is the plan?"

"You have been brought here to fulfill a certain task."

David had not expected that answer. What could they possibly do that the alien artificial intelligence could not? Or were they being kept as objects of study for the sphere's consciousness, as proxy for humanity?

"What kind of task?"

"I am not authorized to impart that information. You will be informed later, together with your companions."

"Not authorized?"

"No."

"But you are the AI, aren't you?"

"That statement is only partly correct. I am an element of the network. But my scope is limited and I have only one specific purpose."

"Which is?"

"To make your arrival more pleasant, help you to acclimatize, and answer your questions. I shall consider that duty fulfilled as soon as you leave this room. Another representative will take care of you after you have met with your companions."

David swallowed the last bite of his sandwich and rubbed his hands on his pants. "Then I'd like to be taken to them now."

The other man nodded and stood up. "Follow me." He reached for the doorknob, hesitated, and turned around again. "Behind the door it will not be as you expect."

David nodded. "I already figured." Again, he looked the man with his father's face in the eyes from up close. Again, he was fascinated by the perfect resemblance. He even thought he could smell the spicy note of his father's aftershave. "Will we see each other again?"

The other man shook his head. "No. My task will have been completed as soon as you leave this room. I will reas-similate with the network."

It was an interesting statement, but it wasn't what David was asking. "I meant, will I see my real father again?"

The other man smiled wanly. "I do not have any infor-mation on that set of issues. I am unable to answer that question."

David nodded. "Yeah, alright."

The other man turned back toward the door and opened it. A shining white brightness entered the bedroom. David took a deep breath and crossed the threshold. The door closed behind him.

Chapter 2

It really wasn't what David had been expecting. He had known it wouldn't be his parents' hallway, but he had formed an idea of what it would look like. If the alien wasn't lying and David was inside an asteroid, he'd thought he'd enter some kind of rock tunnel, or a futuristic hallway like the inside of a space station. But this? He was in a corridor, but it was neither futuristic nor cave-like. Instead, the white walls and strip lighting on the ceiling were reminiscent of a shabby hospital or doctor's office. Along the wall in front of him were four gray plastic chairs. Next to them stood a white water dispenser. David took a few tentative steps. The hallway ended after only a few yards. Not until now did David realize that there were no other entrances. The only way to leave the corridor was through the door he had just exited.

On a whim, David turned around, quickly returned to the door and turned the knob.

"What the—?" he blurted. The door was locked and didn't budge an inch. He was trapped! David suffered from claustrophobia, and he felt a familiar panic rising up inside him. But he remembered the therapy he'd had during his astronaut training and was able to calm himself down. There was no way they had brought him all the way here just to keep him forever in this bizarre hallway. Finally, he went over to the chairs, sighed, and took a seat. In this environment, he actually felt like he was waiting for an examination. Really, he just wanted to see his friends. The doppelgänger had said he would bring him to them. So where were they?

David closed his eyes and tried to relax. The wooziness and his headache were gone. He even felt rested, and the meal had revived him. Maybe, he speculated, the orange juice had contained more than just vitamins.

He replayed the encounter with the doppelgänger in his head. His welcome had not been inhospitable. The sentience had gone to the trouble of reconstructing his father and his childhood room, just to ease David's recovery. Its behavior was nothing like the impersonal chill with which the sphere had communicated with them on the Helios. But why the drastic destruction of their ship while they were still on board? If the artificial intelligence wanted something from them, it could have brought them to this asteroid right away. Why wait until they were unconscious and half dead? And how had it even gotten them off the Helios? The more he thought about it, the more questions he had and the less answers. On the other hand, the doppelgänger had suggested that they would be informed about everything when the time came. Still he'd like to know why ...

David felt a slight breeze and tore his eyes open. The door at the end of the corridor opened and out stepped ...

"Wendy!" David jumped up and ran to her.

The astronaut's face was swollen and tears were running down her cheeks. Her shoulder-length brown hair was standing every which way. She was wearing the same mission outfit as David. She sobbed, but as soon as she recognized him she opened her arms. The door behind her closed again. David couldn't see who had closed it.

Wendy fell into his arms, weeping. "David." Her voice was pained.

"It's alright," David whispered, stroking her hair. The situation made him uncomfortable, intimacy always did. Whenever he felt sad or scared, his usual response was to retreat. He waited a few minutes, bringing her to a chair after she had calmed down a bit. She sat without letting go of his hand.

"We were dead!" Wendy sobbed. "We died!"

"Looks like we didn't," David said, in a sarcastic tone he immediately regretted. "But it was a close call."

Wendy sniffed, inhaled deeply, and began breathing more regularly. It took a few minutes for her to calm herself. David sat silently holding her hand. Finally, she pulled it away and, trembling, used it to wipe her face. David bent over the water dispenser. He pulled out a white plastic cup and held it under the spout. Filling the cup half-way, he passed it to his crewmate.

"Thanks." Her hands were shaking so badly that water spilled from the cup onto her shirt.

"Better?"

Wendy took another deep breath and then nodded. "A bit." Her voice still sounded pretty teary.

"Who did they send to wake you up?" David asked softly.

"My husband," Wendy answered.

"Gerry."

"I thought I was waking up from a bad dream in our bedroom. My memory came back to me in pieces."

"Same here. I didn't get suspicious until I saw that nothing was moving outside the window."

"I didn't dare look out the window. I was scared of what I might see."

"Their simulation was almost perfect," David said. "What made you suspicious?"

"The way Gerry spoke. So aloof and emotionless. It wasn't like him. As more and more memories returned, I realized I must still be in outer space and whoever that person was, it wasn't Gerry. I was almost surprised that he admitted it right away when I confronted him."

"Where did he tell you we are?" David wanted to know.

"On an asteroid. But he didn't want to say where."

"What do you mean?" David had assumed that they were in orbit around the sun somewhere close to the sphere.

"I thought it was strange that they would put us on an asteroid belt inside the sphere."

David smiled wanly. "There are asteroids throughout the solar system, not just in the asteroid belt."

"Even so far out? Beyond the sphere?" Wendy asked.

David nodded. "Of course." Then he hesitated. "Actually, we don't call them asteroids then, we say TNOs."

"TNOs?"

"It's an acronym—transneptunian object," he explained. "It's weird that our hosts didn't use the correct term, they're usually so precise." Were they really still near the sphere? The truth was, they didn't have a clue.

"The being I was talking to didn't bear much similarity to the artificial intelligence of the sphere. At least not what we saw of it."

"I think the doppelgängers just acted the way they did

to go easy on us. I'm pretty sure we'll be dealing with the old Q again soon."

"What do you think they want with us?"

David shrugged his shoulders. "I can only guess, but I bet—"

Again, the door opened. David and Wendy both stood up. David knew who would be crossing the threshold any moment now. And he was right. Pale and wide-eyed, but poised, Grace strode into the hallway. With her mission outfit, her red hair in a short bob, and the freckles around her nose, she looked like she had just stepped out of the propulsion module onboard her beloved spaceship. She stood still for a moment, looked around, and headed straight for David and Wendy. Wendy walked toward her to give her a hug, but Grace waved her away. "Please, just leave me for a sec ..."

She walked past them and sat down on the farthest chair. "Just for a minute," she added, her voice hoarse.

Wendy sat down next to her, but made no attempt to touch her. Her gaze alighted on the fourth chair. "Who's that for?"

"I assume it's for our host," David replied.

"You mean they're going to send us another of those ... people?"

"I don't know. It would make communication a heck of a lot easier."

"How do they even do that? How do they create those doppelgängers? Are they real people? Clones? Robots? Made of nanomachines maybe? Or holograms?"

"No idea. They're definitely not holograms. I touched my father's double and he felt like a real human being. But I don't think they're clones."

"Why not?" Wendy asked.

"That would mean they cultivate doppelgängers just

for one conversation, and then destroy them. Even if they could accomplish that at such short notice, the moral implications are staggering."

"And the alien intelligence is just a bundle of scruples," Grace snapped.

David leaned over and looked her in the eyes. She seemed to have gotten over her shock. "Actually, I think the aliens do have principles. They don't necessarily match our moral values. But at least they saved us from the wreckage of the Helios."

Grace snorted. "But Ed is dead. They killed him. Don't tell me the aliens have morals!"

David shook his head. "Ed died because he drifted into the stream of antimatter exhaust. It was an accident."

"Which only happened because the aliens jammed our controls. Q allowed us to die out there."

"But they didn't. They saved us."

Grace gave a short laugh. "They told me they have a task for us. So they only rescued us for their own ends."

"Who was with you?" Wendy asked. "Who was there when you woke up?"

"Kathy. My partner."

David nodded. "When did you realize what was going on?"

"I didn't. She told me. First I thought she was pulling my leg. Then my memory started to come back." She sounded mad.

"Did they tell you anything more about our task?"

Grace blinked. "Why *they*? Is it singular or plural? We should maybe decide that."

David shrugged his shoulders. "Probably both are right. The network of spheres as a whole would be singular. If we mean the sphere around our sun, that's also singular. But since the intelligence can split itself into multiple instances, as we saw with the doppelgängers, we can also use the plural."

"Let's just stick to the singular," Wendy said. "Whether or not other spheres exist and it splits into elements or incarnations or whatever, we're still dealing with the intelligence of the sphere around our sun."

"I can live with that. 'It' it is then," David said and turned back to Grace.

"So? Did it tell you any more about this ominous task?"

The engineer shook her head. "No. We'll find out the rest soon, they—I mean *it*—said."

"Alright. Then we'll just have to wait until it feels like finally showing itself."

"We won't have to wait long," Wendy sputtered.

David spun around. She was right. The door had opened again. Somebody cursed. David's jaw dropped. He recognized that voice. And he had been sure he would never hear it again. From inside the room, a shadow approached the doorframe and stepped into the light.

Wendy screamed.

"Ed!" Grace whispered.

Chapter 3

"What kind of bullshit is this?"

That was the first thought to enter Ed's consciousness upon waking. He groaned and rasped: "Bullshit!"

His head was about to split in two. But he forced his eyes open. They were stuck together and he blinked. He could hardly make anything out for all the sleep in his eyes. He did at least register that he was lying on his belly on a bed. Summoning all the resources of his maltreated body, he turned onto his side. Again he groaned.

In front of him was a model of a space shuttle, a digital clock in its base. He knew that thing. He had bought it himself for under ten dollars more than twenty years ago at the Kennedy Space Center gift shop. It had been his alarm clock ever since. That meant he was at home and, as he had thought, in bed. Light from the window flooded the room, ergo, it must be daytime. A second glance at the clock told him that it was shortly before nine thirty. But why did he feel so awful? His head felt like it was about to explode into a thousand pieces and his stomach rumbled as if he'd spent the night drinking everything in the bar. That must be why he felt so terrible. Why couldn't he remember anything? He had no idea what the occasion had been or how he had gotten back home. What day was it even? He didn't give a thought to whether he was maybe missing work because of his hangover. Like many astronauts, he could party hard, but he was disciplined enough to never overdo it when he had to work the next day.

Still, something was wrong—he'd never had a blackout like this.

"Coffee?" a voice on the other side of the bed asked.

Ed jumped, startled almost to death. He recognized Helen's voice of course, but some vague intuition told him she shouldn't be here.

He rolled over onto his other side with difficulty. "Helen!" he said, his voice hoarse. His wife was sitting on the rickety wooden chair she used to lay out her clothes in the evening. Ed usually left his own clothes in the bathroom. He felt under the blanket and realized he was wearing underwear. Normally, he went to bed naked, which Helen had teased him about more than once over the course of their long marriage.

Helen was wearing designer jeans and a fashionable blouse in various shades of brown. Her hair was done up carefully, like she had just come back from the hairdresser. She looked at him with an expression full of curiosity. "Are you OK, Ed? How do you feel?"

"Awful," he answered, honest as always. "What happened? I don't remember a thing."

"You were sick," his wife answered.

Sick? Yeah, that made sense. Maybe food poisoning. That would explain his headache and the queasy feeling in his stomach.

"Coffee? You want breakfast?"

Ed wasn't sure he could keep down solids. On the other

hand, he was hungry. "That'd be great, hon," he said, not very convincingly.

Helen got up and went to the door. "You'll find something to wear in the closet."

"I don't want to get dressed. I think I'll just spend the day in bed. We don't have plans today, do we? Don't tell me I have to work!"

"No, you don't have to work. But some friends want to see you."

Friends? At most he had colleagues. Other astronauts with whom he was continuously vying for the best missions. Probably it was people Helen worked with from one of her charities. None of them were his friends. "They can kiss my ass and come later," he groaned.

"It'd be better if you got dressed now," Helen answered calmly, but with an air of authority that Ed seldom heard from her. Wasn't the best idea to waste the whole day in bed, anyway.

"Aye, aye, Ma'am," he replied and pulled back the bedcovers, while Helen slipped into the hallway.

Ed groaned again as he sat up and swung his legs out of bed. He raised his arm and realized that he was trembling. Sitting on the edge of the bed, he stared at the back wall of the bedroom. Next to the wardrobe was a painting of flowers, a watercolor in soft pastels. Ed made a face. He'd wanted to hang a painting of the moon by ex-Apollo astronaut Alan Bean, who had started a career as an artist after retiring from NASA. But Helen would not put up with any space-travel memorabilia in her bedroom. Except for the alarm clock on the nightstand of course, which Ed had put there in an act of resistance.

Slowly he stood up. He had to steady himself on the mattress, otherwise his knees would have buckled and he'd have hit the floor. He groaned as he made his way to the oak wardrobe at the back of the room. He swayed back and forth on his heels unsteadily, until he was sure he could stand without falling. At least his headache was a little better and he could think halfway clearly. What was wrong with him?

Instead of Helen's usual array of garments, only one shelf had any clothes on it. He pulled the pile out and was surprised to see that it was an astronaut's outfit. His? But he didn't recognize the color, which changed with each mission. He shrugged. At least it was something to wear. He threw the top on the bed and pulled the pants on clumsily. Then he reached for the rest and unfolded it. A mission logo was sewn onto the breast pocket.

The Helios mission!

His memory returned like an explosion. His stomach cramped and he began sweating. His legs gave way under him. He fell a few steps backwards and landed on the bed.

I'm dead.

The realization hit him like a hammer.

I must be dead!

He remembered the explosion of heat and pain when he had fallen into the antimatter jet on his spacewalk. He was dead! How could he be here in the bedroom of his home in Houston? It wasn't possible. And Helen shouldn't be here either; she'd left him before the mission started.

Ed began to tremble even more. He glanced around frantically.

Where am I?

Was he dead and this was the afterlife? A new form of hell created by his dying consciousness, which had doomed him to spend eternity with an illusion of his wife?

No!

This couldn't be death! It went against everything he believed in.

Another memory returned, and in a split second he understood what was going on.

The door opened, and "Helen" entered. Ed couldn't see what was beyond the doorframe, but it was very bright. The door closed. The woman put down the tray on the small round wooden table next to the door. "Your breakfast, Ed."

"You bastard!" Ed trembled, with rage this time.

The woman turned around. She didn't seem the least bit surprised. "Your memory has returned," she stated calmly.

"You're not Helen," Ed screamed, jabbing a finger at her. "You can't be. You're the AI!"

"Your conjecture is correct," his wife's doppelgänger confirmed without emotion. "The return of your memory and capability for logical deduction suggest that your awakening process has been successfully concluded."

"My awakening process?" Ed barked. "I almost died. Goddammit! I really thought I had died!"

"You are alive. That's what counts."

"Tell me where I am immediately! Where are the others? Where is the Helios?"

The doppelgänger smiled Helen's smile. "Slow down. One thing at a time. As to your first question: You are inside an asteroid. Second—"

"Inside an asteroid? Are you serious? I'm in my own fucking bedroom! I ..." Ed balled his hands into fists and took a deep breath. He had to calm himself, though God only knew how.

"Second," the other Helen continued, "the others are very close by. As soon as you have calmed down, I will bring you to them. Third, the Helios has been destroyed. Do you have any other questions for me?"

The Helios destroyed! His spaceship, that he had

commanded, which he was responsible for ... Destroyed! By this alien intelligence, that had prevented them from contacting Earth!

"Why? Why in God's name did you destroy our spaceship?"

"Because you failed to follow instructions and instead damaged the sphere."

"We were prisoners on board our own spaceship. By not letting us return to Earth, you sentenced us to death. Of course we tried to save our butts."

Helen nodded. "Yes, that was a logical consequence. We expected that reaction."

Ed snorted. "Like hell you did! We burned a hole in your stupid sphere and sent a message to Earth. The human race knows about you now and won't rest until you've been terminated. This is our solar system—we're not going to sit around and let you confine and observe us like animals in a zoo."

"I have to disappoint you," the doppelgänger retorted, without a trace of triumph in her voice. "Your message never reached Earth. I did say we had been expecting your reaction."

Ed closed his eyes. If she was telling the truth, every-thing had been for nothing. Or had it? They *had* to warn humanity about the presence of extraterrestrials at the outer reaches of the solar system. What had the AI said? They were on an asteroid. Then they must have brought him and the others here somehow. Which in turn meant there must be a spaceship somewhere. Maybe they could capture it and fly to the other side of the shield. Then they could still get a message to Earth. But first the AI would have to think there was no danger ...

Ed opened his eyes. "We're in an asteroid?" he asked, his voice almost friendly.

Helen's doppelgänger nodded. "Yes."

"Where are the others?"

"They're waiting for you outside."

"Then bring me to them!"

The doppelgänger remained in her chair. "You must still be very weak, and also hungry. Eat some of your breakfast first." She pointed to the tray.

"You can put that where the sun doesn't shine," Ed shouted. "I've lost my appetite."

"I insist."

Ed opened his mouth to give an appropriate retort, but he realized he actually did need to eat something. Finally he sighed, stood up, and lumbered over to the small table. Without sitting, he picked up a glass of something that looked like orange juice and drowned it in one gulp. Then he reached for what seemed to be a turkey sandwich and ripped off large bites, swallowing impatiently.

"Can we go now?" he asked, his mouth still half-full.

The Helen clone shrugged, got up, and went directly to the door. "Your friends are waiting right outside. You will be picked up shortly and provided with further information about your task."

Ed's mouth fell open. "Our task?"

The doppelgänger nodded. "Yes. You have been brought here for a very specific purpose."

Ed hadn't thought about that yet. Of course. The aliens could have just left them to die out there. There must be a reason why they hadn't.

"What task?" Ed asked skeptically.

"You will find out as soon as you are picked up."

Ed just grunted while the woman opened the door. It was so bright, Ed had to blink. He stepped over the threshold and almost tripped, his legs were still very weak. A loud expletive escaped his lips.

"Ed!" cried a voice he immediately recognized as Wendy's. He stepped into a hallway and his crewmates jumped up from a row of chairs. Wendy ran to him and he groaned loudly as she hugged him hard. "Ed!" she cried again.

He patted her on the back. "No need to get all excited," he said. She stepped out of the embrace and took a step back to Grace and David, who stood open-mouthed.

"I didn't expect to see you guys again," Ed rasped.

"You were dead," David murmured. "We saw it. You floated into the middle of a stream of antimatter."

Ed looked down at himself, hit his chest with his fist, and shrugged. "Looks like I'm not dead. The aliens must have somehow protected me and brought me here."

David shook his head. "No. We saw it. We even *felt* you going into the antimatter. The radioactivity from the explosion penetrated the skin of the Helios—it triggered the alarm! Based on all the evidence, you *must* be dead."

Ed groaned. For him, it was a clear-cut case. He was alive, so he couldn't be dead. "So, smarty-pants, how do you explain the fact that I'm standing right in front of you?"

"I can't," David answered, with a dry inflection that Ed hadn't thought him capable of.

"But the same is true for us," Wendy interjected. "We should be just as dead as Ed."

"I guess we'll find out exactly what happened when the alien finally comes to get us," David said.

"And I'd really like to know what's happening on Earth," Grace added. "There's that atomic war Q told us it wanted to observe. You think this 'task' has something to do with that?"

"I don't give a shit about its task," Ed growled. He felt himself getting angry. The alien had sabotaged and destroyed their spaceship and almost killed them. What right did it have to give them some job now? It was a glaring injustice! Ed wasn't going to rest until he had found a way to get back to the other side of the shield and warn humanity. "No matter what, we have to get out of here somehow and make contact with Earth. We have to ..." Ed wished he could bite his tongue. Why was his mouth always faster than his brain? Of course they were being watched; now he'd aroused the alien's suspicion.

"I want to hear what the alien has to say first," David said. "Then I've got a whole bunch of questions I want to ask. Also—"

"Looks like you're about to get your chance," Ed interrupted. The door had opened again. They all stared at it expectantly.

A man stepped out of the shadows and over the threshold. He was a strange sight. Of medium height, he had a mass of black hair streaked with gray that had been hastily combed back. His clothes looked they were from a past century. He wore a white shirt with a loosely knotted tie under a brown and beige checked tweed jacket that looked like a flea-market find. His pants were made of the same fabric, and he wore brown leather shoes. The man had a friendly smile that was partly hidden by a large black moustache. His brown eyes twinkled and he waved as he walked toward them.

David gasped for breath.

Ed shook his head. The man looked really familiar. He almost looked like—

"Einstein," the stranger said politely, with a German accent. "Albert Einstein. It's a pleasure to meet you."

Chapter 4

The only word to describe the situation, thought David, was "bizarre." Here they were, four people who had believed themselves dead inside an asteroid on the outskirts of the solar system that looked like a 1980s hospital hall-way, or sometimes like their own bedrooms. And now the renowned genius Albert Einstein was standing right in front of them. Or at least his doppelgänger was. Since Einstein had died in 1955, David had of course only ever seen photos of the man, but the resemblance was so uncanny, it took his breath away. The famous physicist had always been one of his greatest role models. Was he just one of the simulations sent by the alien? Or had also he risen from the dead, like David himself? Hesitantly, he stepped forward and reached out his hand; "I'm David Holmes," he said.

Einstein smiled and took his outstretched hand. David got goose bumps. The man's handshake was not very strong and his palms were decidedly damp. He was most certainly not a hologram.

"It is a pleasure to make your acquaintance," the Nobel Prize winner answered.

"You're not Einstein," Ed said brusquely. "You're just another illusion! A robot made of nanomachines or what have you. Created by that artificial intelligence!"

Einstein looked at Ed. "If you say so," he answered in the same friendly voice. "You must be Ed Walker. I've already been informed about your uncooperative behavior."

Ed just grunted.

"And I must say, I like it," Einstein added with a mischievous smile.

"Oh do you?" Ed retorted.

"We have something in common. I never did have much respect for authority."

Wendy took a step forward and touched Einstein's suit. "Are you the real Einstein?"

The physicist's smile faded and the furrows in his brow deepened. "That is a very good question," he said slowly. "It is in fact a question that I have also asked myself. I have many memories of my life on Earth …" His eyes filled with tears and David got goose bumps again. "And yet I know that that life is over and that I am merely here to fulfill a task."

"What kind of task?" Grace wanted to know.

"To show you the way, to instruct you, and accompany you."

"What *way*?" Ed asked. His voice dripped with disparagement. It was obvious he believed Einstein was a cheap trick by the AI, brought here to manipulate them. "You were sent by them, weren't you?"

Einstein nodded. "Yes, I am working on the behest of the network. It is my task to show you the way."

"You said that already," Ed retorted. "So what do want us to do?"

"You will be informed bit by bit in the coming hours, while I fill you in on the complex background. I would like to start by saying that it is an extremely important and momentous mission."

A mission! The choice of words did not go unnoticed by David. So it wasn't something they could do from this asteroid. They were going to be sent somewhere. But where? And to do what? "Can't you give us a little more detail?"

Einstein nodded. "Certainly. Follow me, and we can begin."

Without waiting for an answer, the physicist—or his doppelgänger—turned and walked to the door. He opened it, and stepped inside. David followed him over the threshold without hesitating. "This was my bedroom a minute ago," he said in admiration. Now it was another hallway that mirrored the one they had just left. Only this one was longer and there were more doors in the white walls.

"Where are you taking us?" Ed asked warily.

"Wait! Your curiosity will soon be satisfied." Einstein stopped in front of one of the doors, opened it, and stepped inside.

David followed right behind; the room was very dark in contrast to the hallway, and it took his eyes some time to adjust to the shadows. It could have been the conference room of any random company. In the middle stood a large rectangular table surrounded by a half-dozen black leather chairs. White plaster wallpaper covered the walls and a large television hung at one end. Across from the door was a row of windows, darkened by metal blinds.

David shook his head again. There was nothing here to

suggest that they were in the interior of an asteroid. The extraterrestrials had clearly spared no effort to create an environment that would feel familiar to humans. But maybe it was no effort for them to transform the asteroid's interior.

"At least turn on the light," Ed complained.

Einstein shook his head. "No. I'd like your eyes to adjust to the dark."

"For what?" Grace asked.

"For this," Einstein answered, and pressed a button on the wall. Silently, the blinds slid up.

David walked to the window. His eyes gradually became fully adjusted to the dark and he stared into the infinity of space. Stars spread out in front of him, forming a veritable carpet. But … he shouldn't be able to see this stellar ocean.

Surprised, David turned to Einstein. "Why are there stars everywhere?"

"Not everywhere," Grace replied. "Look to the left!"

David gazed out of the window again and started. The engineer was right. He hadn't noticed, because he hadn't been looking in that direction. On the left-hand side was only darkness, like a line had been drawn down the stars with a ruler.

"What's going on here?" Ed asked, taking a step toward Einstein.

"You are intelligent people," the physicist said, and smiled. "You should be able to work out the answer to that question yourselves."

David turned away from the window and went a step closer to Einstein. "I don't understand. We're outside the sphere, so we shouldn't be able to see any stars. And if we're being held inside the shield, then the whole sky should be full of stars, not just half of it." He thought feverishly. "Have your friends begun to dismantle the sphere?"

Einstein laughed softly. "No."

"Then what's going on?" David asked.

"Review the assumptions that your hypothesis is based on," Einstein persisted, and smiled.

"My assumptions?" David wasn't aware of having made any suppositions. He'd expressly left it open whether they were inside or outside the sphere. They couldn't be ... Suddenly, an idea came to him and he broke out in a sweat.

"Oh my God!" David swiveled to look again at the starry part of the sky. He tried frantically to make out a constellation, without success.

"What?" Ed asked. "What's the matter? Are we outside the sphere or not?"

"Outside ..." David squawked.

"So how come we can see the stars?" Grace wanted to know.

"David," Ed urged. "Talk to us!"

"You've gone so pale," Wendy said.

David walked to her and put both hands on her shoulders. "We're not in our solar system anymore."

Her eyes widened.

"They've brought us to the limits of their zone of influence." He pointed to the dark half of the sky. "That's where their nanomachines have built Dyson spheres around every single star. Somewhere in that blackness is our sun, surrounded by a shield that sucks up its energy for their computer simulations."

Ed shook his head. "We're in another solar system? I can't believe that!"

"It's the only explanation."

"But we established on board the Helios that the aliens

had enclosed all the stars in our galaxy with Dyson spheres," Wendy exclaimed.

David nodded. "Right. The next galaxy we could see, that hadn't been completely darkened, was M87." He turned to Einstein. He barely dared to ask the question. "Where are we?"

The physicist's face, which until now had almost consistently sported a slight smile, was absolutely serious. He looked each one of them in the eyes before he spoke. "We are in a dwarf galaxy that has never been charted on Earth." The short pause seemed endless to David. "About eighty-one million light-years away from your solar system —and from Earth."

A deathly silence fell over the room.

The news superseded David's wildest conjectures. His mouth agape, he stared out of the window at the light of stars that had never before been seen by human beings.

"You've mastered faster-than-light travel," Ed concluded in awe—his sarcasm vanished in the face of this new information.

"That is correct. Around one million years ago we found a way to travel through space at speeds faster than light."

David tried to take in the new information. He had always assumed that the aliens hadn't broken the light barrier. If they had, their spheres may have spread throughout the universe even faster.

"But why did you bring us here?" Wendy asked. "Why to the edge of your sphere of influence, of all places?"

"It has something to do with this mission you want to force us on, doesn't it?" Ed conjectured.

David pulled himself away from the window just in time to see Einstein nod. "That is correct. We want you to fly out there." He pointed to the sea of stars. "It's an exploratory mission. You will learn the details in due course."

"An exploratory mission with a spaceship that flies faster than the speed of light?" David asked.

"Yes, that is correct. But as I said, you will learn more later."

David lifted his hand. It made no sense. "Just to clarify. You brought us here in a spaceship that defies the speed of light and now——" He broke off when he noticed Einstein was shaking his head.

"I did not say that you were transported in a spaceship."

Ed looked at him blankly. "Then how …?"

"It's a process that you call 'quantum teleportation.'" Einstein tittered. "I used to think it was impossible."

"Quantum teleportation?" Ed asked doubtingly. "You mean, we were beamed here like in *Star Trek*?"

"I've read theoretical and practical inquiries into the topic," David said. "Zeilinger's in particular. But they were always on the transmission of information, not mass. Not at all like teleportation in science fiction." One thing in particular was bothering him. "In the experiments on Earth, the original atoms always had to be destroyed in order to transfer the information to others."

Einstein smiled. "Smart kid. And you are of course right: At the moment of your deaths, your corporeal information was transferred, quantum-mechanically, to the raw material found here, by means of entanglement."

"At the moment of our deaths?" Wendy repeated breathlessly.

Einstein nodded. "It is a fundamental principle of physics: in quantum teleportation, the original must be erased. Otherwise you could produce copies."

David felt increasingly anxious. "I've remembered

something else from the papers about the process," he said hoarsely. "Despite the quantum process, to prevent an information paradox, actual transmission cannot be faster than the speed of light."

Einstein smiled. "Also correct."

Now David's whole body was covered in goose bumps. His stomach contracted. "But that would mean ..." He couldn't finish the sentence.

Einstein nodded. "Yes, that is right," he said quietly. "Since you left your solar system, eighty-one million years have passed."

From the corner of his eyes, David saw Grace grow pale and collapse.

Chapter 5

"Bullshit!" Ed screamed. "It's nothing but fucking bullshit!"

"Can you please calm down?" Wendy said, her voice devoid of emotion.

"I don't want to calm down," Ed screamed, but a little more quietly.

After Grace had fainted, Einstein ended the meeting and brought them to their quarters, Ed carrying their crewmate. Their rooms were along the white hallway. The sparse furnishings reminded David of nothing so much as a cheap hotel room. In his stood a bed with a white blanket and a flower-print bedspread. Next to the bed was a wooden chair and desk, and a standing lamp. A frosted-glass door led to a small bathroom. The only thing missing was a TV. There was a closet with some clothes; all identical copies of the mission outfit and the white underwear. The first thing David did was to take an ice-cold shower. Then it hit him and he broke down.

Eighty-one million years!

His parents, his friends, everyone he'd ever known! After that much time, even their dust would be gone.

After minutes that seemed like hours, he pulled himself together, got dressed, and crossed the hall to the common room. It was a bit larger than their sleeping quarters. In the middle stood a round table with four chairs. On one wall was a small cooking area and a fridge. David was surprised to see it was stocked with Coke. They must have found a way to synthesize that, too. He grabbed a can and sat down next to Ed who was perched on one of the chairs brooding over an unopened can of beer. A few minutes later, Grace and Wendy entered, got themselves something to drink, and joined them.

"Can it be true?" Wendy asked. "I mean, eighty-one million years?"

David nodded. "I'm afraid so. It makes sense. "We're definitely at the edge of their zone of influence. Otherwise we couldn't see the stars."

Wendy sobbed. "Everyone we know. Gerry! My parents! All dead. For millions and millions of years."

Grace walked over to her and began to massage her shoulders. "Eighty-one million years," she whispered. "It's a number too big to grasp. I keep trying to imagine what Earth looks like now. How has humanity changed? I don't even know where to begin."

"Of course not," Wendy said, her voice still full of tears. "Neanderthals were still alive only thirty thousand years ago. The first ancestors of humans and chimpanzees lived six million years ago. Eighty million years before our time was the Cretaceous Era. There weren't even any advanced mammals yet—dinosaurs still roamed the Earth!"

"Fucking bullshit," Ed murmured.

"But Einstein said they're putting us on a faster-than-light spaceship," Wendy said. "Why only bring us here at the speed of light."

"He also said it was 'only' one million years ago they broke the light barrier," David answered.

"They brought us all the way here to a faraway galaxy in a far-off future so that we can go on a spaceship mission for them." Ed looked each of them in the eyes. "That's going to quite a bit of trouble, and it's a pretty long development period for a mission. No matter how important or difficult. Which brings us to a completely different question."

David looked up. "Which is?"

"The aliens control the stars of innumerable galaxies. With their network, they have a computing capacity humanity can only dream of. They're more powerful than the Gods of most of our ancestors. So," Ed tapped his temple, "why the fuck do they need us for some mission that they could probably get their nanomachines to do a thousand times better."

"I haven't the slightest," Grace answered.

Ed looked at David. "What about you?"

David figured the question was rhetorical. He shook his head.

"I'll tell you why. There's only one possible answer. First: They finally met another species that can hold a candle to them—"

"That's pretty farfetched," Grace interjected.

Ed ignored her. "And now, they need us as soldiers for a suicide mission!"

David shook his head. Farfetched was putting it mildly.

Grace laughed out loud. "Looks like your imagination's gotten the better of you."

"So let's hear your theory," Ed said coldly.

"I don't have a theory," she answered. "I already said: I don't know. We'll find out from Einstein soon enough."

Wendy cleared her throat. "Speaking of Einstein. What do you think of him?"

"How do you mean?" Grace wanted to know.

"Is he *the* Einstein?" Wendy sounded unconvinced.

"The real Einstein is dead!" Ed retorted with conviction.

"They might have scanned him before he died and brought him back here, like they did with us," Wendy said.

"I get goose bumps just thinking about it, Grace whispered. "Imagine what else the aliens can do! If that's the real Einstein, maybe they scanned everyone who ever lived before their deaths. They might all be quantum signals floating in space, ready to be awakened one day by a superior intelligence."

"That's what our religious friends think is going to happen, in any case," David said.

"I fail to see the similarity with the Christian belief in resurrection," Ed retorted. David knew his commander was not only politically conservative, but also a god-fearing man. "I'm not buying it. I think this Einstein is a simulation."

"But he seems so ... so human," David said quietly. "He even shows emotions."

Ed rolled his eyes and raised both hands. "Simulated or risen from the dead, I don't get why they've given us Einstein of all people. Like they're trying to impress us."

"Ask him the next time we see him," Grace proposed.

"Oh I will," Ed answered with a cold smile.

Chapter 6

Ed peeked furtively around the corner. Any minute now, Einstein would emerge from behind the mystery door bearing a tray with bagels, muffins, and breakfast sandwiches. He always came at the same time: a quarter to seven. At least that's what the analog clock above the common-room door said. Einstein would put the tray down on the table and then disappear again.

The common room, their bedrooms, and the meeting room, all connected by the hallway, were the only places the human crew could access within the asteroid. The door through which Einstein came and went was locked. Ed wanted to know what was behind it.

He heard the familiar sound of the lock and pulled his own door shut, leaving it open a sliver. He waited until Einstein's silhouette passed his room and he no longer heard steps, then ran down the hallway until he reached the door Einstein had come through. Ed stuck his hand between door and lock just seconds before it closed. He reached for the doorknob and pulled the door open again. A quick glance back down the hallway showed it was still empty. The famous physicist's doppelgänger was in the common room, where he usually stayed for only a few minutes. By the time he came back out, Ed needed to have found a place to hide.

He crossed the threshold and entered another hallway, much darker than the one in their area. He couldn't really tell where the light was coming from. The corridor was narrow, but long—it went at least one hundred yards before it disappeared around a corner. There were no other turn-offs or doors he could see, meaning no hiding places.

Ed inspected the door. There was a knob on this side and he made sure he could turn it before letting the door shut. Then he ran lightly to the end. Before the turn he stopped and glanced slowly around the corner. This section of the hall was also empty. It turned another corner at the end, and halfway along there was a door on the left-hand side.

He looked behind him again—Einstein would be back any second, he had to find a place to hide. He ran to the door, hoping whatever was behind it would offer cover.

The steel-gray door had neither knob nor handle. He pushed it carefully and it moved easily. It needed even less force than he had expected, considering how heavy it looked. He slowly pushed it open a tiny bit and peeked inside. The space was small; it looked like a storage room. But whatever used to be kept in it, it was empty now. He heard steps coming down the hallway and slipped into the room. Before Einstein turned the corner, he had the door closed, leaving it open just enough to see the physicist pass by a moment later. Maybe Ed could find out where he was going. There must be more aliens around here somewhere. After all, one doppelgänger couldn't do everything alone.

Ed waited until Einstein's footsteps receded and then

slipped out again. He crept cautiously to where the hallway veered off at a shallow angle. Peeking furtively around, he caught a glimpse of Einstein walking through a door, which closed silently behind him. The corridor itself went quite a bit further than the door, ending at a two-way junction.

Ed crept to where Einstein had vanished, taking great care not to make a sound. The door had a knob and was made of the same gray steel as everything else here seemed to be. Should he take a chance and open it? What if Einstein was standing right behind it?

Ed pressed his right ear to the door. Silence. If he wanted to know what Einstein was up to, and what was going on here, he was going to have to take the risk.

Carefully, he reached for the knob. He suppressed a groan, because he could neither turn the knob nor push the door open. But maybe he could find out something else of interest. The asteroid had to have some kind of machines or equipment. Maybe a control room, or a hangar with spaceships. He couldn't believe that the only way in or out of here was quantum teleportation.

He tiptoed to the junction. To the left was an incredibly long corridor that ended somewhere far away. The walls of the right-hand corridor were dotted with doors. Maybe he could open one of them. At the junction, he stopped for a second and looked back the way he had came. He just hoped he didn't get lost. For all he knew, the whole complex was one giant labyrinth. The best thing would be to somehow mark the turn, but he didn't have anything suitable on him. Ed sighed and ripped a small piece of fabric from his blue outfit. Bending down, he placed it as far as he could reach down the hallway he had come from. It was the best he could do.

Turning around, he went to the first door. He reached

for the knob.

Locked!

He tried the door across the hall, but it was also locked. If it went on like this, he might as well turn back now. It figured. They'd been here for days already, inside a barren rock in the universe's bumfuck nowhere, and Einstein still hadn't told them what the hell was going on or what the aliens wanted them to do. It was time for somebody to do some straight talking. What was Earth like now? What about humanity? And most of all—what was this all about?

Ed swore under his breath on his way to the next door. This one had no knob, but opened easily when he pushed against it. He stepped inside and had to stop himself from gasping loudly.

Ed gazed around the enormous room in amazement. It was larger than a football field and the ceiling was so high that a three- or four-story building could easily have fit inside it. But the biggest surprise was the view of outer space, which spread out in front of him—with no wall or window to obstruct the view. But since he was still breathing, there must be some kind of force field or invisible pane. The room was reminiscent of a hangar.

Ed took a few steps towards the gigantic opening and stretched out his hand. He felt the resistance right away. It was cold, like a windowpane in winter. But he couldn't say whether it was some transparent material or a force field.

He looked around some more. Maybe it was a hangar. But then where were the spaceships? The machinery? The equipment? There was nothing at all here. The walls were smooth and unadorned and seemed to be fabricated from the same gray steel-like material that everything here was made of. The whole place was weird. Like an unfinished shell that had been abandoned before it could be turned into something useful. But that couldn't be the case, because it had an atmosphere, warmth, and light—and every day Einstein brought them something to eat. There had to be more. Machinery, storage rooms, a mission control, *something*. Obviously, he hadn't found it yet.

Just as he was turning to leave, he noticed a glowing patch at the front of the room. Stepping closer to inspect it, he saw that it looked like a small switchboard. A red light was blinking, below it were two orange areas and one blue part.

He furrowed his brow. If it was a control panel, it was the weirdest one he'd ever seen. He couldn't make out any switches or indicators. The lights looked more like they were projected onto the wall, and he couldn't see anything that looked like writing. Maybe it was a main switch meant to activate other systems. Impulsively, he reached out his arm and pressed the red light.

All hell broke loose.

Ed felt a hard blow to his back, and another to his chest that pressed the air out of his lungs. His eyes were suddenly burning, and he had to squeeze them shut. He felt like he was falling, but he didn't hit the ground. And he was freezing cold, like someone had pushed him into a refrigerated room. What had he done? He gasped for breath, but there was no air to breathe. Panic flooded his body with adrenaline.

Ed forced himself to open his eyes. He was surrounded by darkness. He was spinning in outer space, the stars twirling faster and faster around him. From the corner of his eyes, he saw the asteroid rapidly growing smaller. And while he lost consciousness, he realized what he had done.

You idiot, you opened the airlock!

It was his last thought before darkness covered him like a blanket.

Chapter 7

Ed screamed while he fell.

"Ed, wake up!"

He heard Wendy's voice and realized that he was no longer falling, but he kept on screaming.

"Ed!"

Ed sat up quickly, opened the eyes, and was quiet. Wendy's face was directly in front of him, David and Grace were right behind her. In the background, Einstein was leaning against a wall. Ed lay in his bed, wearing only underwear again. Had he had a nightmare? No, the images were too clear.

"What happened?"

"That's what we wanted to ask you," Wendy answered gently.

"I was falling," Ed said. "I must have activated the airlock by mistake and fallen out of the asteroid."

Einstein pushed in front of David and Grace. "You left the living quarters and entered an equipment airlock. And, in fact, opened the door. You have the asteroid's automatic fast-react to thank for saving your life."

"Automatic? You beamed me back on board?"

Einstein shook his head. "No. A transport robot grabbed you and you were reanimated in the sick bay."

"How long was I out there?" Ed asked. His voice was still hoarse, and he cleared his throat.

"About eleven minutes."

Ed's eyes widened. "Eleven minutes?" he gasped. "Eleven minutes without oxygen? No one can survive that!"

The medical advancements of the builders of this asteroid surpass yours by far. They are able to regenerate damaged brain matter. At least to an extent." It was hard to overhear the sarcastic undertone of the last sentence, and Ed had to grin despite his critical situation.

"How long was I in the sick bay?"

"About an hour."

"That all happened only one hour ago?"

"Correct."

David stepped to the front. "You said: 'the builders of this asteroid.' You didn't make it habitable yourselves?"

Einstein shook his head. "No. The asteroid belonged to a species that lived in this galaxy. They wanted to colonize other parts of their Milky Way. We're just using their infrastructure."

"And what about the people? Where are they?" Wendy asked.

"Disappeared."

David furrowed his brow. "Disappeared? "What's that supposed to mean? Interstellar species don't just disappear."

"When our nanomachines arrived in this galaxy and installed the spheres, we found the remains of this civilization everywhere. Their physical and mental makeup was not unlike that of humans, by the way; we know this from recordings we found. But their technology was considerably more advanced. Never found a trace of the beings themselves though. It was as if they had vanished."

"An illness maybe? Some kind of plague?" Grace guessed.

"Unlikely. We did not discover any corpses. We have not yet found an answer to this question that can be considered more than pure speculation."

"And you just took over what they had left behind?" Ed was slowly feeling himself again.

"Yes. To our surprise, we found the technology for faster-than-light space travel, which we were interested in using." Einstein paused. "Needed to use."

"Here," David guessed. "In this asteroid."

"Here and elsewhere. This asteroid was one of the species' research stations. It was where they experimented with manipulating gravitational fields. Many of the sectors in this asteroid are dangerous." He looked accusingly at Ed. "Which is why we did not give you permission to leave your living quarters."

That was no reason to lock them in. Ed opened his mouth to say something, but contented himself with grumbling to himself.

"How large is the asteroid?" Grace asked.

"Around six hundred miles. Most of its volume was hollowed and set up for various purposes. The total length of all corridors, passageways, and rooms is over one point two million miles."

"Damn!" Grace exclaimed.

Einstein nodded. "Should you get lost, you would never find your way back, but spend the rest of your life walking through the asteroid. Another reason we have forbidden you to enter other areas."

"I don't like being locked up," Ed explained.

"I noticed," Einstein replied. The physicist's smile as he said it almost provoked a very obscene reply from Ed.

Instead he inhaled and exhaled deeply. It's not like it would help them. "When are you finally going to tell us what we're doing here?"

Einstein bobbed his head. "Your impatience is amusing. I wanted to give you some time to regenerate. Teleportation across such distances is torture for every organism. Not to mention the psychological burden for intelligent beings. But so be it. I will provide you with the details of your mission today. It's more of an expedition actually. You will depart in a faster-than-light spaceship to take measurements in an area beyond our zone of influence."

"What kind of measurements?" Ed asked tersely.

"As I have told you, you will learn the details very soon. It is an eminently important expedition that concerns the fundamental aims of our existence. It is in your own interest to cooperate."

"And if we don't?" Ed retorted.

"Participation in the expedition is of course voluntary, although your refusal would be lamentable. We have created living quarters for you on this asteroid as an alternative. But you would not be allowed to leave them."

Ed laughed out loud. "You call that voluntary? The mission or a life sentence here?"

"However, should you decide to participate and return successfully with the measurements, I shall return you to your solar system."

"Does humanity still exist?" Wendy whispered.

Ed swallowed.

Einstein looked at each one of them in turn, and then nodded. "Yes."

A chill went down Ed's spine. What were human beings like now? Had they taken the next evolutionary steps and developed a superintelligence, as some visionaries had predicted? Or had humans degenerated, reverting to semi-intelligent animals after an atomic war? Then they would return to Earth as gods.

"It would be great to have some more information," Grace said evenly. "About humanity as well as about the mission."

Einstein shook his head. "I am unable to say more at this time. I will leave you alone now. Your mid-day meal is in your common room. I expect a decision by dinnertime."

"First you leave us hanging and now you want a decision within four hours?" Ed glared at Einstein. "Even though we have no idea what it's about? Are you kidding me?"

Einstein stopped in his tracks, his hand on the doorknob. "It is because of you."

"Me?" Ed asked, surprised.

"You have shown that it is better not to leave you alone for too long. Total surveillance such as we can conduct within the sphere around your solar system is impossible here. We have therefore decided to push the timetable forward. We expect your answer by this evening."

He disappeared through the door.

"Asshole," Ed swore, after the door had fallen shut.

"From the volume of your voice I conclude that you are feeling better," Grace stated.

"I'm fine. Never felt better," Ed replied.

"Can't you think before you act?" the engineer continued. "That almost cost you your life."

Ed swung his legs out of bed, holding on to the edge of the mattress as he stood up. "I wanted to let you guys know, but I didn't know whether or not they're listening in. I thought it couldn't hurt to have some more information."

"Without, apparently, considering the cost." Grace

snorted. "Did you ever stop to think what would happen to *us* if you bit the dust out there?"

David grabbed Grace's arm. "Stop fighting, that won't get us anywhere. We have more important questions to answer. If nobody has any more objections and Ed's feeling well enough to get dressed, I say we go into the kitchen, sit down at the table, and discuss this expedition."

Ed shrugged, let go of the mattress and stumbled forwards. "Then let's get going!"

"I WONDER where they get the cold-cuts," Wendy said, closing her sandwich again. "Or any of the food. It tastes like they just bought it at the corner deli."

"I'm sure it's synthesized," David said, biting into his burger.

"But it tastes so real," Wendy said.

"Maybe they rebuild it, atom for atom. They must have the recipe, or blueprint or whatever you want to call it, in some database about our culture."

"A recipe that's millions of years old ..." Wendy said quietly.

Ed rolled his eyes. He'd sat down and was slowly sipping a glass of water. The events of the morning had stolen his appetite. "Can we please just get onto the subject at hand? Are we going on the aliens' mission or not?"

"What do you think?" Grace asked.

"I've already said what I think. I'm not interested in doing their dirty work."

"So what's your alternative? Escape?"

He shrugged. "Beats me. I don't have an alternative." He thought for a while. "Escape? In what? And more importantly, where to? But I still don't want to take their measurements for them. They spied on us, isolated us, killed us, and brought us back to life just to snatch us and take us millions of years through time and space. And now we're supposed to do their bidding?" Ed shook his head. It went against everything he believed in. But what other choice did they have?

"I don't think we have a choice," David said. "If we don't go, they'll lock us up in some remote sector of the asteroid with enough supplies to last a lifetime and then throw away the key. It really would be like a life sentence in prison."

"There's no such thing as an inescapable prison," Grace reminded them, but she didn't sound very convinced.

"Yeah," said Wendy. "But even if we got out we'd be still be inside this rock. And even if we somehow managed to hijack a spaceship ... where would we fly to? Earth? The aliens would be waiting for us."

Ed sighed. There was nothing they could do. "You're right. I want to return to Earth and find out what's become of human beings. Looks like the only way we'll ever get there is to complete the aliens' mission. Let's do it."

Wendy nodded. "I'm in. I can't think of a better solution."

"David?"

The physicist also nodded. "Agreed."

Ed turned to Grace. "What do you think?"

She stared in his direction for a long time, but her gaze went right through him. "OK," she finally said.

Chapter 8

"You can't imagine how happy your decision makes me," Einstein said. "You have made the right choice." I think this is a good occasion for a little treat." He reached into the inside pocket of his plaid jacket and, to David's great amazement, pulled out some thin cigars. He held one out to Grace, who quickly shook her head. David and Wendy also turned him down. Ed looked skeptically at the famous man. "They're Turkish!" Einstein said.

Ed took one of the small cigars and eyed it suspiciously. Einstein put one into his own mouth and stuck the rest back into his inside pocket. Fishing out a box of matches, he handed them to Ed. Ed checked to make sure the end had been capped, and stuck the cigar between his teeth. Then he lit a match on the striking surface, held it to the cigar, and puffed.

Einstein did the same with his own. "Good, aren't they?" he asked, after a few puffs. Some of the smoke floated in David's direction, making him cough.

Ed shrugged. "First cigar I've had since back when I was a test pilot." He examined the glimmering object from all sides. "And this is really supposed to be from Turkey? I have my doubts."

Einstein reached into a drawer and extracted a glass ashtray, which he pushed in Ed's direction.

David shook his head. The situation was bizarre. Here they were inside an asteroid, hundreds of millions of light-years away from Earth and just as many years into the future, and Albert Einstein was offering them Turkish cigars.

David turned his head and stared out the window at the stars. Einstein had called them into the meeting room. David was burning with curiosity. Finally they would find out what this ominous mission, which they had now agreed to go on, was all about. "Can't we have a few more details now?"

Einstein stared at him thoughtfully, puffed again on his cigar and nodded. He placed the burning end of the tobacco in the ashtray. "Certainly. Allow me to go back a bit."

Ed sighed.

"You remember the reason the spheres were created?"

David nodded. "Yes. How could I forget that conversation with Q. You wanted to create a new universe, since our own is unstable. You needed the network of spheres to calculate the solutions to some important equations. In the end, they're like parts of an intergalactic network of mainframes."

Einstein smiled. "Couldn't have put it better myself."

"So what's all that have to do with this expedition?" Ed asked. He sounded impatient.

"Everything," Einstein answered, still smiling. "We have solved the equations."

David was impressed. "You mean you can create a new universe?"

"Yes. The solutions to the field equations provide us with the necessary information about the metrics we need beyond the event horizon."

Ed rolled his eyes.

"Beyond the event horizon?" David asked. "You're going to create a new universe out of a black hole?"

Einstein nodded. "More or less …"

"And the new universe will be stable?"

Einstein smiled again. "That's exactly where we've run into a problem."

"What kind of problem?" Wendy asked.

"We don't know which boundary conditions to use."

"Boundary conditions?" Ed asked.

"Yes. We know what we have to change in relation to our own universe, but we are still missing some fundamental parameters. We tried the standard default options, but they didn't work. So we have planned expeditions to measure the missing parameters. You will receive a spaceship, fly to the coordinates we give you, and get the values we need to continue our work."

"Your work?" David said. "As in: building a new universe?"

"Correct," Einstein answered. "We cannot put it off any longer. We must hurry."

"Hurry?" Ed asked. "What for? You've waited billions of years, another couple of million shouldn't make any difference."

"That's where you are wrong," Einstein answered. "The death of the universe is imminent."

David felt his stomach cramp. "The death of the universe? What do you mean by 'imminent'?"

"You are familiar with the process of vacuum decay?" Einstein asked.

David nodded. "Rudimentarily. I know that our

universe consists of a false vacuum. At any time it could transition to a new aggregate state with a lower energy level, like a lake that freezes in winter. Q said it would happen instantaneously—that the whole universe freezes at once."

"The word 'freeze' is just an analogy," Einstein said.

David nodded. "Yes, of course. At any rate, the natural constants of the entire universe would change from one instant to the next. Matter—including life as we know it—would no longer exist." He inhaled deeply and slowly exhaled. "And this is about to happen soon? How do you know?"

"The fundamental constants have already begun changing. We noticed a few years ago, during a routine inspection of the fine-structure constant, that it had altered slightly. As had the speed of light, the Schwinger limit—and even the gravitational constant and some masses of elementary particles. The universe has left the metastable state and is slowly rolling into an increasingly deeper abyss."

"But—"

Einstein raised his right hand. "We are in luck; the transition is taking place gradually and has produced signs. But it will accelerate."

David saw that both Wendy and Grace were wide-eyed. Even Ed seemed shaken. The hand in which he held his cigar hadn't moved.

"How long do we have?"

"We don't know exactly. It might be another ten years. But if the process accelerates, it might only be a couple of months. At some point, the gluons will no longer be able to hold the quarks together, and the hadrons will decay. Which will mean the end of matter in this universe."

"... the world was formless and empty," Ed whispered,

"darkness covered the surface of the watery depths. And the spirit of God hovered over the surface of the water."

"Huh?" Grace asked. "Is that from the Bible?"

Ed nodded. "Genesis 1:2. If Einstein is right and all matter in the universe vanishes, we'll return to whence we came: the void ..."

"Not quite," Einstein said. "We have calculated that the new vacuum will have a negative cosmological constant. Whatever remains after the decay will fall toward a final singularity in which even space and time will cease to exist. Nothing will even hint at this universe ever having been here. None of the achievements of humanity or any other species will remain, not even as a memory."

A long silence ensued. David stared out the window. The stars of a faraway galaxy still twinkled. But they would do so only for a few more years. David closed his eyes, he felt dizzy. It was one thing to know that you were going to die. But that there would be nothing left at all! All memories, all proof of his existence—gone! It was simply unimaginable. And the alien intelligence was the only way out. David opened his eyes again. "You still want to create a new universe?"

Einstein nodded.

"And bring your knowledge to it?"

He nodded again.

"You've also saved humanity's legacy? You're going to transport it to this new universe?"

"Yes. We will."

Actually, there was no need to think about it. David would do whatever he could to help the extraterrestrials. He could see from Wendy's and Grace's faces that they felt the same. He would have to talk to Ed. "And you need our help to execute the plan?"

Einstein nodded. "I have already said so."

"What should we do? What measurements do you need?"

"We require the topological parameters of our universe."

"I'm afraid I don't—"

Einstein raised his hand. "We'll need to know the exact form and scale of our universe if we want to build a new one."

"You mean k, the curvature parameter?"

"Exactly."

"Hold on a second," Ed interrupted and turned to David. "You've lost me. They want us to conduct measurements that have to do with the structure of the universe?"

"That's how I understood it," David answered, happy to see that Einstein was nodding.

"And what does 'curvature' mean here?" Ed asked.

"According to the theory of relativity, matter and energy bend space-time. A heavy mass like our sun curves space to such an extent, it even diverts light waves. Cosmologists assume that the entire universe is curved due to the matter within it, but there's disagreement about its exact form." David looked at Einstein. "But you must have learned more by now. In comparison to human knowledge …"

Einstein gave a wan smile. "We have determined local curvature parameters that suggest a finite topology, but we still don't know the exact shape."

"Could the two of you please speak English?" Ed asked. "Are you trying to say the universe has limits?"

"I am saying that the volume of space is limited," Einstein answered.

"That's what I said!"

"No, you asked whether the universe has limits." David thought he heard the physicist snickering.

"Same difference!" Ed mumbled.

"Imagine you were walking across Earth," Einstein explained patiently. "Would you hit a physical limit?"

"Of course not. If I went straight ahead, at some point I'd be back where I started."

"A sphere does not have physical limits?" Einstein asked with a smile.

Ed tilted his head to the side. "No?" he muttered hesitantly. "No," he repeated, with more conviction.

"Is the surface of the Earth finite or infinite?"

"Finite," Ed said.

"Same with the universe. It is finite, without having any limits. We presume that the universe has the form of a hypersphere."

Ed nodded slowly. "I think I'm beginning to understand. You're saying if I leave with a spaceship, at some point I'll return to where I started."

"And our mission is to fly faster than the speed of light and at a certain distance measure the curvature of spacetime?" David asked.

"Correct," Einstein answered.

"How far should we fly?" David asked.

"The whole way!"

David squinted at him. "What whole way?"

The Nobel Prize winner drew a circle in the air with his finger and grinned. "You will orbit the universe until you have returned to this point."

Chapter 9

"If I didn't know better, I would say it was a bad joke," Ed said. He stood up and got a bottle of beer out of the fridge. Without alcohol, sadly. What he wouldn't give for a bottle of good scotch right now!

After their talk with Einstein, Wendy requested a break. They went back to the common room, where a heated discussion began immediately.

"I don't think Einstein was joking," David replied. "I'm sure he meant just what he said!"

"Circumnavigate the universe," Ed groaned. "That's the stupidest thing I ever heard!"

"If human beings had discovered faster-than-light travel, I'm sure somebody would have tried it at some point," Grace put in.

"Never. Who would be so stupid?"

"As soon as sailing ships were sturdy enough, people started trying to sail around the Earth."

"Like Columbus?" David asked.

"But he failed, and only discovered America," Grace

answered. "The first person to successfully sail around the Earth was Magellan."

"Wrong!" Ed interjected loudly. He remembered a book on famous expeditions that he had read some time ago. "His crew made it, Magellan himself was murdered by natives on the Philippines."

"How big is the universe, actually?" Wendy asked. As a biologist, she'd never had a head for physics.

David shrugged his shoulders. "Nobody knows."

Ed raised his hand. "Wait a second," he said. "If I remember correctly, the universe is about fourteen billion years old."

"That's right," David answered.

"So if nothing can move faster than light, its radius can't be larger than fourteen billion light-years," Ed said triumphantly.

"Fourteen billion light-years!" Grace whispered.

David shook his head. "Sounds logical, but I'm afraid it's wrong."

"And why, pray tell?"

"It's true that the light from the farthest reaches of the universe needs about fourteen billion light-years to get to us."

"That's what I said!"

"Yes, but it may have expanded since then. Because of the theory of relativity, it can't be directly converted. Those regions of space are now forty-five billion light-years from Earth. The total circumference of the observable universe has been calculated at about ninety billion light-years."

"So we'll have to travel ninety billion light-years?" Ed asked. He didn't even know how to begin thinking about a distance like that.

David shook his head. "That's just the observable universe. Also known as the Hubble volume. Meaning the distance which light from the creation of the universe needs to cover to reach us. But there might be regions beyond that which just haven't made it to us yet, because there hasn't been enough time since the Big Bang. The universe could be a lot larger."

"How much larger?" Ed asked.

David hesitated. "Who knows … ?" He finally answered.

"Those numbers are unimaginable," Wendy said. "What kind of spaceship with what kind of propulsion system could they possibly have to get us across distances like that?"

"You will be surprised!"

Ed jumped. He hadn't heard Einstein come in.

"If you like, I can bring you to your spaceship."

Ed stood up immediately and turned to the others. "Let's go."

Einstein led them from their living quarters through the normally locked door and down the long corridor Ed knew from his excursion. The physicist strode purposefully, making many turns until Ed had lost all sense of direction. Finally they reached a ramp that slanted down sharply. Einstein stopped and gestured for Ed to go first.

Ed looked down the ramp skeptically. It was at least a forty-five-degree incline. And the end was pretty far away. If he lost his balance, he could break his neck. "That's pretty steep. Your friends could at least have put in a handrail."

"Let's see what you're made of," Einstein challenged him, and grinned.

With a sigh, Ed took a step forward. His heart froze as he stumbled. He must have miscalculated, any moment now he would fall … but after the next step he was standing as securely as if the surface were flat. He turned around, surprised. "What the hell is this?"

Einstein and his crewmates looked like they were standing at a bizarre angle on a ramp going down.

"Is this what I think it is?" Ed asked.

"I do not know what you are thinking," Einstein replied, "but here the artificial gravity changes its vector."

"There's artificial gravity on the asteroid?" David asked.

"Of course," Einstein answered. "Its mass is not great enough to generate a sufficiently large natural field of gravity."

"I should have realized that," David said, and took a step toward Ed. He also stumbled as his body swung forward unnaturally, and he almost lost his balance, but Ed caught his arm.

Einstein chivalrously helped Wendy and Grace over the invisible threshold and the group continued on their way. "The beings that lived in this galaxy were no more advanced than we are, overall, but they are the only known species to have mastered the manipulation of the gravitational field. We use their technology, but we have yet to completely understand its theoretical basis."

"Nice to hear there's something you can't do," Ed said.

"Yet the alien race became extinct," Wendy reminded them.

"Maybe," Einstein replied, "maybe not."

"What do you mean?" Ed asked. "Can you please stop talking in riddles?"

"Possibly they did not become extinct, but rather also noticed that they were living in an unstable universe. One of our hypotheses is that they created their own universe and relocated."

"Did you find anything to suggest that?" David asked.

"No. They disappeared without leaving any indication of their destiny."

Einstein led them down more passageways with more turns, stopping before a metal door that looked exactly like all the others here. He touched the wall and then simply pushed the door open. Walking behind Einstein, Ed stepped into a large room similar to the hangar-like space from which he'd been catapulted into space. A transparent wall gave a fantastic view of the stars. Einstein stepped aside, allowing Ed to see the center of the room. There, hovering over the floor, was a spaceship. Its silhouette was more than familiar.

"Unbefuckinglievable!" he cried, taking two steps forward. "It's the Helios! You brought her here!"

"No," Einstein replied. "Your Helios was destroyed at the edge of your solar system. This is a reconstruction from our scans. With some modifications."

"Why do that?" Ed asked. He was flabbergasted. He'd expected the advanced alien intelligence to design some futuristic spacecraft—the intergalactic equivalent to an aircraft carrier or some such. Something that looked like it could actually get all the way around the universe. Not the Helios, which had been pieced together from remaindered ISS modules and looked for all the world like garbage cans that had been welded together.

Ed took a step to the side. Only now did he notice the change. "You added a module," he said, pointing to the silver cylinder next to the antimatter propulsion unit. It was attached at a right angle to the connecting node and was about as long as the Habitat module.

"That is the faster-than-light propulsion module. Another, smaller, module flanges the connecting module on the other side and contains the sensors you will need for your mission," Einstein explained. "We used the Helios as a model, since it fulfills its purpose and you already know it so well."

"How does faster-than-light propulsion work?" David asked eagerly. Ed was perhaps not quite as curious as their scientist-astronaut, but he also wanted to know. It could hardly be rocket boosters. His guess was that they somehow manipulated gravity.

"It uses a modification of the space-time metric developed by the builders of this asteroid," Einstein said, confirming his suspicion. "The spaceship exists in a kind of bubble that contracts the space in front of it and expands the space behind it. Although the spaceship seems to stand still within the bubble, it is propelled forward at speeds faster than light."

"I always thought nothing could move faster than light," Ed replied, staring skeptically at Einstein.

"That is correct. Nothing can move faster than light." He grinned at Ed. "That was, after all, my postulate. But there is one exception. Space-time itself can move at any speed. May I explain with a thought experiment?"

"Be my guest," Ed replied.

"A person cannot run faster than, say, twenty-five miles an hour."

"If you say so."

"But when running inside a fast train, they can go much faster, even when standing still. Or, to give another example, when a beetle——"

Ed raised his hands. "I think we get it."

"I've heard of the principle," David said. Ed wasn't surprised. The kid was generally pretty up to date. "We call it Alcubierre warp drive, but it's a purely theoretical construct. Similar to wormholes, more energy would be needed to curve space-time than is available within the entire universe."

Einstein nodded. "Yes, according to my theory of relativity, that is true. But it does not account for quantum effects."

"I know," David answered. "You yourself spent the rest of your life searching for a unified theory."

"Which we have yet to find to this day. But we have been able to approximate the solutions to special cases. The builders of this propulsion system also found a special solution. It takes most of the energy needed for the local curvature of the gravitational field from the effects of the curve itself."

David laughed. "Sounds like you've invented a perpetual motion machine."

"No," Einstein replied. "The expansion of space-time behind the spaceship is minimally smaller than the contraction in front. The energy comes from the vacuum itself, by destroying a minuscule bit of space in the process."

David ran his hand through his hair. "You draw energy from the destruction of space?"

Einstein nodded excitedly. "Yes, it makes no difference, since space expands with the universe anyway. The metric does not lose anything, it simply expands more slowly in one locality."

"Can we skip the science and get to the practicalities?" Ed asked.

"Of course," Einstein answered politely.

"If we're going to circle the universe, that spaceship must move pretty damn fast," Ed said. "So how fast can it go?"

"Infinitely," Einstein answered drily.

"You're pulling my leg," Ed replied.

Einstein shook his head. "Not at all. The propulsion

works with increasing speed. The longer it is activated, the faster the spaceship goes."

"So how long will we need to circle the universe?" Wendy asked.

"If the circumference is ninety billion light-years, around two months. Including the braking phase at the end."

"And if the universe is larger?"

"As I said, the propulsion speed is not constant, but accelerates continually. Should the universe be nine hundred billion light-years across—or ten times larger— you would need only a few weeks more."

Ed shook his head. The whole project was simply insane.

Chapter 10

"Weird not to be weightless on board the Helios," Ed said, letting himself into the commander's seat. He studied the consoles carefully, and was happy to see all the controls exactly where he expected them to be. The aliens had replicated the original almost to a T. For all he knew, they'd done it atom by atom. He just hoped Einstein and his friends hadn't fucked up at some crucial juncture.

"We had gravity on our flight to the outer solar system, too," David answered from his seat behind Ed.

"But the vector was different," Wendy added. She was sitting in her old seat behind Ed and turning her monitors on. "During the acceleration phase, the vector pointed in the direction of the tail, where the boosters are. Here it points to the side, like in the simulators on Earth."

"That's only because we're in the hanger now," said Einstein, who was standing between Ed and Grace. "When you leave the asteroid you'll be in zero G."

"No artificial gravity?" Ed asked, feigning disappointment. But he'd always loved weightlessness. He'd found it made his work easier, especially aboard the ISS.

"No," Einstein answered. "That would be too complicated."

"Who's the fifth seat for, by the way?" David asked.

Ed turned around, surprised. He hadn't noticed the small seat when he'd entered the bridge. It had no consoles and was dwarfed by the array of equipment at David's station.

"For me, of course," Einstein answered, and laughed.

"You're coming with us?" David asked.

"Is that really necessary?" Ed muttered.

"I'll be here to help and support you all the way," Einstein said. "Besides, I know the ins and outs of faster-than-light propulsion and the sensory equipment module, in case there are ever any problems or questions."

"If the propulsion unit stops working, we'll be stuck forever in some far-off part of the universe," Wendy said, and shivered.

"Unlike now," Ed retorted.

Grace groaned. "Ed, could you give us a break from the running commentary for once?"

Ed shrugged and scrolled through the monitors at his console. He still felt like he was trapped inside a B-movie. Circle the universe ... Where was the hidden camera?

"Primarily, I'm coming along as an observer. Bet even if the sensors do record everything, it is possible that my personal opinion will be needed on our return," Einstein said.

Ed snorted.

"While I cannot help but noticing you do not trust me, I have only your best interests at heart." Einstein smiled brightly.

Ed laughed out loud. "If you had our best interests at heart, you'd have let us go home to our families."

Einstein looked at him for a while, and finally nodded.

"I can understand that you are angry about that. But please don't blame me, I did not make that decision."

"Oh, and who did?"

"The answer to that question would surely be the cause of much alarm."

Ed groaned and turned back to his control panel. There was no sense in continuing the conversation. He began activating the spaceship's systems. That was actually Grace's job as flight engineer, but he wanted to take a look for himself. Scrolling through the status reports, he started. "You refilled the antimatter stores!"

"Yes," Einstein confirmed. "Faster-than-light propulsion is not suited to local maneuvering."

"So how do we steer it?" Ed asked.

"Can we just stick to 'warp drive' instead of 'faster-than-light propulsion'?" David suggested.

"Warp drive?" Grace repeated.

"Yes, space-time is warped in both directions and the spaceship rides in between—in a kind of bubble, as Einstein said."

"OK by me," Ed said. "And how do we control it?"

"Grace has a control panel on her console," Einstein explained. "It's very easy. She can turn the bubble on or off and also accelerate or decelerate."

"And where can I check the warp drive?"

"That will not be necessary. The whole system operates independently."

"And if something breaks?"

"You would not know how to repair it," Einstein answered.

"Well then, that solves that problem," Ed commented drily. But something else was bothering him. "I have one more question."

Einstein stared at him. "Yes?"

"If you're coming with us anyway, and you know everything better than us lowly humans ... why the hell not just take your own spaceship to measure the universe if you need the numbers so badly? Why be such assholes and drag us dozens of galaxies away from home and dump us in a ridiculous model of our junkyard spaceship to do your work for you? Can you explain that to me?"

Einstein gave a wan smile. "That's a good question. I would have provided the answer on my own in due course, but if you insist, why not now?" He took a deep breath. "We tried that—we sent off an unmanned network of probes, put together by nanomachines."

"And?" Ed asked.

"And none of them returned. They disappeared after crossing the horizon of the observable universe."

Ed stared at Einstein for some seconds in silence. Then he broke out in loud laughter.

"Would you mind telling me what's so funny?" Einstein asked, seeming angry for the first time since they'd met him.

Ed tapped the physicist on the chest with his finger. "You are!" he answered, still laughing. "You know what this reminds me of?"

Einstein just raised one eyebrow in answer.

"Of our first flight with the Helios. From Earth to the outer reaches of the solar system, where our own probes had stopped sending signals. Thanks to you and your sphere. There's a certain comic justice in it—even with your superior intelligence, you're in exactly the same predicament."

Ed laughed loudly again at his next idea. "And who's behind it now? Some even more powerful assholes, who've maybe put a sphere around the entire universe?"

He slapped his thigh, but he was the only person on the

bridge who seemed to find the situation amusing. Grace's lips were pressed firmly together and Wendy was shaking her head. David and Einstein just stared at one another in silence.

"What's wrong with you guys? I for one think it's very funny."

"I fail to see the humor," David said seriously. "You've forgotten that the universe itself is at stake. If our mission fails, humanity's legacy is lost."

Ed snickered. "Humanity's legacy! Please! Even if Einstein here transfers everything the sphere has recorded to a new universe, what good will it do us? You think that in some future time, in some future universe, some new species will appear and find those recordings? That's ridiculous!"

"It's not that improbable," Einstein replied. "We want to make sure that in the new universe, all species have access to all recordings. With the genetic code, they could even create humans."

"And how do you want to accomplish that?" Ed asked. "Send millions of storage devices into the newly created cosmos?" He laughed again.

"No. At the birth of the new universe we'll code our datasets in an irrational number."

David turned pale. "You can do that?"

"Of course, you only need the right initial conditions at symmetry break."

"What's an irrational number?" Wendy asked.

"A mathematical constant like Euler's number, the basis of natural logarithms."

"Not my field," Ed said impatiently.

"Euler's number is 2.71828182845 and so on. The sequence seems like it's completely random. If you manage to manipulate a natural constant, you can hide a quasi-infinite dataset within it. Every inhabitant of the universe would see the message as soon as they reached a certain mathematical maturity. Pi is another such number, by the way."

"That's crazy!" Wendy said.

"Not really," David replied. "Some of our researchers also spent years searching for hidden messages in irrational numbers."

Ed snorted. "Like God would hide his messages like that."

"It could be that our cosmos is only the creation of an older intelligence from another universe. But you can rest easy. No one ever found the Bible or the Koran or anything else in the numbers. David looked at Einstein. "Or did you find something?"

Einstein shook his head. "No."

"A different answer would have surprised me," Ed said. "But we've gotten off track. We were talking about your probes that never returned. I got that part right?"

"Yes," Einstein answered.

"Why do you think they stopped sending signals? Give us some more information! What kind of probes were they?"

Einstein sighed. "They were nanomachine networks in the form of a sphere about thirty feet in diameter. They contained both warp drive and the necessary sensors. We sent many off, in all different directions. None of them ever returned."

"So why should we succeed where your probes failed?"

"The intelligence of the probes was limited. Maybe living beings are better suited to the task, due to their capacity for intuition and improvisation."

"And if we also just disappear?" Ed asked.

"We've developed new experimental technology that

will continuously send measurements to the asteroid. Even if something goes wrong, the network should still receive valuable data."

"Even if we don't survive?" Ed asked.

"Our lives are unimportant in relation to the larger issues at stake."

"If you can't appreciate the small things, you'll never value the large ones."

Einstein looked up and was about to retort, but Ed waved his hand. "Forget it."

"Did I understand correctly?" David asked. "By 'continuously send measurements' you mean some kind of faster-than-light communication?"

Einstein nodded. "Correct. A submicroscopic wormhole creates a permanent connection between the spaceship and this asteroid to send your data to our computers."

"You developed that technology?"

"No," Einstein answered. "Like warp drive, we found it in the legacy of the vanished alien race."

"Wouldn't it make more sense to first send out new probes with the new technology before sending a manned mission?"

Einstein shook his head. "Even after we receive the data it will take years before we are able to create a new universe. As I said, time is running out. We cannot afford to wait any longer. We will have to take the risk!"

"When do we start?" David asked.

"As soon as possible. Since you are already familiar with your ship's systems, there is no reason to wait long. You will have four days to inform me of what you will need for the trip, then we can leave. Food for the duration of our travels is already on board."

"Four days?" Ed screamed. When he was working for NASA, they'd taken months and sometimes years to plan routine missions to the ISS. And the aliens wanted to prepare something of this magnitude in just a couple of days? On the other hand, Ed had no idea how long Einstein and his cohorts had already been brooding over this.

Einstein ignored Ed's outburst. Instead, he turned to David. "There is one more thing you should know."

Ed pressed his lips together. How could there possibly be any more surprises?

"You're not the only species being sent on this trip."

David shook his head. "What do you mean?"

"Representatives of all races that we have ever come across have been brought to similar asteroids," Einstein informed them. "They have all been given spaceships and will be leaving on identical missions within the next days. Over six hundred in all."

Ed was sure he had heard wrong. "Six hundred? You're kidding!"

Einstein ignored him. "Even if only one succeeds, we will have saved our cultural legacy."

"And if not?"

"Then all has been in vain and not one intelligent species will remain that remembers our cosmos and its inhabitants."

Chapter 11

"Nice to see a colleague in the morning," Einstein greeted David, entering the lab module from the Helios's connecting node.

David jumped at the words. He still wasn't sure whether or not he was dealing with a doppelgänger, since, like Q, Einstein sometimes referred to himself as "we," as if he were part of the network. But wasn't he still at least partly the famous scientist? Hadn't he said he could remember things that had happened in his life on Earth? And now one of the smartest people who had ever lived calling him "colleague."

"Hi Albert," David answered, turning to face him. "What can I do for you?"

Einstein smiled. His ready smile, together with the mischievous glint in his eyes, made it seem as if he were continuously amused. "Just wanted to make sure that you have everything you need."

David exhaled slowly. He'd spent the past hours hunched over the Helios computers, checking the sensor equipment. He'd been surprised at the similarity to the instruments on their old spaceship. On Earth, even if they had been from the same production, they wouldn't have been as identical. Sensors were sensitive. The new telescope, for example, just like the old one, vibrated slightly at a certain frequency. The aliens had retained all the quirks of the individual instruments when they recreated the ship. As if they had really put it together atom for atom. "I can't find any variance," he said. "I'm very impressed —really."

Einstein nodded in satisfaction and sat down on the stool beside David. In outer space, you had to strap yourself onto the seat with Velcro, or you would float away. "You found the additional modes?"

David had seen them. Scrolling through the menu, he had found new windows, but the fields were all blocked, so he hadn't been able to look at them. "Those must provide access to your sensor module."

"Exactly. As long as we're on the asteroid, the module is deactivated. Once we've started, I'll show you what you can do with them."

David looked over his console again. "But I don't seem to have any way of configuring the sensors."

Einstein smiled again. "That won't be necessary. The instruments are automatic. All you need to do is collect the data."

David shook his head. "No way. Some of the instruments must need to be calibrated. Optics that need to be aligned, apertures that need adjusting—"

Einstein put a hand on David's shoulder, giving David goose bumps. "The module is completely automatic," he whispered, almost conspiratorially. "Trust me."

David nodded slowly. He was glad when Einstein finally took his hand away. "Can I ask one question?"

"Of course, my boy."

"When you discovered the theory of relativity, how did you feel?"

Einstein stared at him for so long, David was about to repeat the question, when the physicist finally sighed. "It was the most wonderful moment of my life. As if God had allowed me to read his mind."

"You remember it?"

Einstein's gaze refocused, and a single tear ran down his cheek. "Like it was yesterday."

"What's the last thing you remember?" David asked. "I mean, before you woke up here."

Einstein seemed to think for a bit. "Pain. An aneurysm burst in my aorta. I'd refused to undergo a risky operation. I wanted to die in peace. Of course I had no idea how painful it would be. Then everything went dark."

David got goose bumps again. He was talking to a man who remembered his own death. If the aliens had simply created a doppelgänger, how would he be able to recall that moment? "And you woke up here?"

Einstein nodded.

"Cognizant of everything that had been discovered in physics and cosmology since your death?"

"Yes, I awoke with that knowledge."

David nodded.

"So now that you're up to date, what do you think of quantum theory now? You never liked it before."

Einstein shrugged. "Neither humans nor extraterrestrials have ever been able to create a functioning theory of everything that applies to all fundamental forces. Until they do, both the theory of relativity and quantum mechanics will remain provisional." The great physicist sighed. He let his head fall and reached inside his jacket. Pulling out a cigar, he put it between his lips and began searching for matches in his other pockets.

"You're not thinking of lighting that in here?" David asked, wide-eyed.

Einstein stared back at him, and then finally shrugged, took the cigar out of his mouth and put it back where it came from. "You are, of course, right."

"How can anyone as intelligent as you smoke at all?"

"Why shouldn't I?" Einstein asked. He sounded very surprised.

"Because it's unhealthy."

"Is it?"

"Yes, of course." David vaguely remembered a TV documentary he'd once seen about Einstein. "Is it true you always bummed tobacco from colleagues?"

"It is. But I did not have much of a choice."

"Why not?"

"My doctor forbade me from buying tobacco."

Chapter 12

"I can't believe we're really leaving to circle the universe tomorrow!" Wendy declared.

Ed looked up from his potatoes for a moment, and then went back to stabbing them with his fork. What could he say? Once more, he would have command of a spaceship; his spaceship. That's all that mattered to him. But it was the most unlikely mission imaginable. *To circle the universe* ... Ed had to laugh out loud at the thought, earning him side-eye from Grace. He had been sure there was no way of one-upping their last mission. If he was honest, his whole life had always only been about one thing: the next mission. Each hopefully more spectacular than the last. If he was going to risk his life, it should at least be worth it. And it looked like his greatest wish was being granted. Nobody was going to top this flight.

But the big question was—what exactly would be waiting for them out there?

"Anybody seen Einstein recently?" David asked. "I'd like to ask him a couple of questions."

"Nope," Wendy answered. "Dinner was waiting on the table when I got here."

"They got the potatoes and veggies right," Grace said. "You gotta hand that to them."

"The food on board won't be this good," Ed posited. He and Wendy had examined the stores that had magically appeared aboard the ship. They looked like the usual plastic-wrapped astronaut rations that NASA used for missions and sent to the ISS. They were edible and, thanks to artificial flavoring, everything no longer tasted the same, like it had back in the Shuttle mission days. But they'd be sick of it after a few weeks, nonetheless. He still didn't have a clue how they made the stuff on the asteroid. But maybe it was better he didn't know. He thought of something else. "We still need a name for our ship."

"It already has a name," Wendy replied. She put her fork down on her empty ceramic plate and pushed it away from her. "Why not just stick with 'Helios'?"

Ed shook his head. "The Helios was destroyed at the margins of our solar system."

"Who cares," Grace said. She forked a potato and brought it to her mouth. "It's not like we don't have bigger problems."

Ed rapped a finger against the edge of the table. "That thing in the hangar is a new ship. It'd bring bad luck to fly under the same name."

"How about 'Terra'? Or 'Sol'?" David asked. "Something that refers to our solar system."

"That's one idea," Ed answered. "I propose 'Endeavour.'"

"The ship in which Cook set off to sail around the world?" Wendy asked. "Sounds good to me."

"Doesn't it?" Ed smiled. He'd actually been thinking of

the Space Shuttle Endeavour, in which he'd taken his first trip to orbit, but there was no need to admit that.

"Or Trinidad," Grace put in. "The flagship in which Magellan actually did sail around the world."

"Sounds Spanish to me," Ed answered.

"What about just 'Magellan'"? Grace proposed. "Seems a fitting way to honor the man."

"It's got a nice ring to it," Wendy said.

"Gets my vote," David chimed in.

Ed sighed. Neither Ferdinand Magellan not most of his crew had survived their trip around the world. But why not? Names are just hollow words after all. "OK, I agree. I —" Ed heard a shuffling step he had come to recognize all too well. "Einstein," he said, without turning around. "Good that you've arrived. We've decided to rechristen the spaceship 'Magellan.'"

Einstein walked around the table. He held a lit cigar in his hand. Wendy waved the smoke away with her hand. "Of course," he said. "A good name. I will have the lettering changed." He pulled up a chair and sat down, putting the cigar directly on the tabletop, where it slowly went out.

"Launch still on for tomorrow?" David asked.

Einstein nodded. "Right after breakfast. The spaceship, I mean the Magellan, is ready for takeoff."

"Do we have an actual flight plan?" Wendy asked. "Or at least a destination?"

Ed perked up his ears. He'd asked Einstein the same question a few days earlier, and the physicist's answer had been evasive.

"Yes," Einstein replied. "We now have a destination. It has been entered into the flight computer. Besides circling the universe, each individual mission has a secondary goal. Ours has now been set and will decide our course."

Ed's heart rate increased. "Secondary goal?" he asked loudly. "That's the first we're hearing about this. It's not exactly standard procedure to change key mission parameters on the evening before launch. It certainly makes planning difficult."

Einstein shook his head. "That's where you are wrong. The missions have all been planned down to the last detail and the parameters were set quite a while ago. But as you know, sometimes you have to improvise in reaction to external conditions."

"External conditions?" Ed repeated. "For example?"

"One of the missions that started a few days ago has been lost," Einstein replied matter-of-factly.

Great

"Lost? What are you talking about?"

Einstein shrugged. "We have lost contact. The microscopic wormhole that we used to communicate with the ship collapsed. That mission had a high-priority secondary goal. We have now taken over the goal and will follow its flight trajectory."

"That's encouraging," Ed grumbled. "But maybe they come back after a while."

Einstein shook his head. "Very unlikely."

"How come?"

"The wormhole connection is also needed for navigation. If it collapses, it's impossible to find the way back. There are at least two billion galaxies in the observable universe alone. Once a spaceship has hundreds of millions of light-years behind it, there are no more points of reference for calculating where it is in relation to where it started from. Returning would be pure luck."

"Very reassuring," Ed replied.

"So what is our secondary goal?" David wanted to know.

"We are to study the Dark Flow."

"The what?" It was clear from Wendy's voice that she'd never heard the term.

Nor had Ed. Einstein turned towards David. "Are you familiar with the Dark Flow?"

David looked at Einstein. "You're talking about that anomalous galaxy drift?"

Einstein nodded. "Exactly."

David ran his hand through his hair. "But that observation was never confirmed. Most physicists just laughed it off."

"Perhaps," Einstein replied. "But we have made the same observation."

"So what is it?" Grace finally asked.

"Dark Flow," David answered, "was observed by a couple of astronomers a while back—must have been around 2008. They found that numerous galaxy clusters in a certain part of space were moving away from us faster than they should be."

"Moving away from us?" Grace asked.

"Just about all galaxies do, due to the expansion of the universe. The further away from us they are, the faster they move. That was Hubble's discovery—which led to the Big Bang theory."

"Can you please get to the point," Ed asked impatiently. He did not want a lecture in cosmology.

David sighed. "At any rate, there must be a reason those galaxies act that way, but we can't discern any with our telescopes. That's why people assume the attraction is beyond the observable universe. Those galaxies are feeling a gravitational pull that ours doesn't. Some scientists even think the pull is coming from overlapping universes."

"And now we're supposed to jaunt over to the horizon,

peek over the edge of the universe and see what's causing the flow," Ed summarized.

Einstein laughed loudly. "All sarcasm aside, yes, that is the plan." The physicist fell silent and looked at Ed seriously. "It might be a gravitational anomaly. It could be incredibly interesting to examine the phenomenon. We might even find weaknesses in my theory of relativity, or something that can point us in the direction of a unified field theory."

Ed groaned. Scientists sure did get excited easily. But he was worried about something else. "Can we get back to that wormhole connection? Especially the part about not being able to find our way back if it breaks down," he said. "Why not just set a telescope in this direction, then we can always see this galaxy?"

Einstein shook his head. "Remember that the universe isn't static. The galaxies rotate, changing both their form and their position. They collide, they merge, they die. When you look back, you see the cosmos as it looked millions or billions of years earlier. Structures in space are as fleeting as foam on ocean waves in a tempest. That's why we set up the wormhole connection. It acts a bit like radio navigation. But if it collapses, we're lost."

There was silence. Ed thought long and hard about what that meant. They were completely at the mercy of a wormhole with an opening that was smaller than an atom. If it stopped working, they were fucked. On the other hand, they were fucked anyway. Ed just didn't like being dependent on technologies and machines he couldn't even begin to understand. On Earth, astronauts were trained in all rocket systems. He could dismantle and rebuild the main engine of the Space Shuttle blindfolded. But not this ship's power source. The warp drive was one big black box and he didn't even know which contraption in the sensor module generated the wormhole. How was he supposed to command a spaceship whose most important components were a mystery to him?

Like it or not, he guessed he was going to have to live with it. But tomorrow at takeoff he would feel less like an astronaut and more like one of those chimpanzees that had ridden in the Mercury capsules. Back when half the boosters exploded at launch.

Chapter 13

"Sensors?" Ed asked. There was no reaction.

"David! Sensors!" Ed repeated more loudly.

David woke up from his daydreams and looked at his consoles. All systems were functioning, although not all were active. "Sensors are green. Go for launch."

"Great! Thanks," Ed answered. "Einstein. What about the artificial gravity?"

The physicist sat next to David, his arms crossed in front of his chest. He had no consoles of his own, but David had not failed to notice that he was always looking over his shoulder. "We will shut it down at your order."

"Then shut her down!"

David suddenly felt like he was falling. He grabbed reflexively for his armrests, but then his brain kicked in. He was weightless.

"OK. I'll maneuver us out of the hangar with the vernier thrusters," Ed told them, and reached for his control stick. Each time the small rocket boosters fired, David was pressed back into his seat. He activated the outboard cameras. The Magellan had exited the hangar and you could already see the dark stony surface of the asteroid.

"Please bring us at least sixty miles from the asteroid before activating the main engines," Einstein requested.

Ed grunted and reached for the control stick again. Using only the positioning system, the commander built up speed. The bright square that was the entrance to the hangar had already shrunk to the size of a postage stamp on David's monitor. But you still couldn't see the whole of the asteroid. You couldn't even tell that the surface was curved.

"Fifteen miles," Ed said. "We'll drift at this speed until we've reached a safe distance."

"Thank you," Einstein said quietly.

Ed turned to Grace. "We'll need another fifteen minutes. Why don't you take the opportunity to check the engine again?"

The engineer nodded and David could see that she was scrolling through the modes on her monitors. He himself used the time to check his own instruments once more. He adjusted the telescopes, aiming for the horizon of the asteroid, which could have been a small planet from its size. He also turned on the spectrometer to determine the makeup of the surface. It showed a bonded oxide with large amounts of silicon, aluminum, and calcium. Although millions of light-years away, the material seemed to be a lot like the regolith that made up the surface of Earth's moon. It even had the same dark gray color.

"Sixty miles," Ed announced. "I'll begin getting the ship into position for firing the main engine."

"The target direction is in the flight computer," Einstein said.

"I saw that. Let's see if this rustbucket can do it on her own. Activating DAP. Program one and confirmed."

David could just see him flipping the switches. The moment Ed turned on the automatic steering, the ship rotated as if turned by an invisible hand, first around its x-axis, then around its y-axis. The movement was slow, but David could feel it in the pit of his stomach. Finally, the ship came to a stop and the stars stood still outside the main window.

"Looks good," Ed confirmed, after checking their direction against the navigation computer. The asteroid is now next to us, that way there's no exhaust in that direction. Grace, you can start ignition."

The engineer nodded and began tapping away on her control panel. "I've programmed a zero point eight G increase in speed. Pre-valves open, injector at operating temperature. Creating magnetic field. Starting in three, two, one …"

David could feel the increasing velocity pushing him back. He readjusted the outboard cameras and watched the asteroid fall slowly away. They were on their way. How far away do we need to get before we can turn on the warp drive?"

"At least two hundred thousand miles. About the distance from the Earth to the Moon," Einstein answered.

"Why so far away?" Ed asked. "Would the artificial gravitational field somehow endanger the asteroid?"

Einstein shook his head. "No. The bubble around the spaceship has a diameter of less than one mile. But the forward movement sends out gravitational waves that could damage the more sensitive sensors on the asteroid."

Ed shrugged. "We should reach that distance in around two hours. Until then, we might as well rest."

David continued flipping through his readings, doing a comprehensive system check. Again and again, his eyes flicked to the image of the asteroid. They were now so far away, it was impossible to see the hangar door. From here, there was no hint that an alien intelligence had hollowed out the celestial body and turned it into a gargantuan space station. If there was an object like that in their own solar system, they never would have found it—not unless some space probe had flown right past it by accident.

A strange grating noise diverted David's attention. He looked to the left. Einstein had fallen asleep and was snoring, his mouth open wide. David couldn't get over how absurd the situation was. Here they were, about to investigate the limits of the observable universe at speeds faster than light, him and his crewmates in blue standard-issue space outfits and Einstein in a worn checked suit that smelled like cigar smoke.

The two hours passed quickly. David had just finished his system check when the thrust stopped and he was again hanging weightless in his seat. Einstein's stopped snoring with a smack of his lips, opened his eyes, and scratched his forehead.

"Engines turned off automatically. All valves are closed. Everything went without a hitch," Grace reported.

Ed patted her on the shoulder, something David had never seen him do. "Great. Then the big moment has come. Einstein?"

The physicist looked up, startled. "What's the matter?"

Ed stared at him. "Everything ready for warp drive?" he asked, like he was explaining something to a child.

"Of course, of course."

Ed sighed and turned to the front again. "Direction is only off by two hundredths of one degree."

What had Einstein said at their last meeting? Once warp drive was activate, there would be no more changing direction. They'd fly straight ahead like a captive balloon until it was switched off again. Only then would they be able to maneuver into another position, and accelerate once more.

"Grace, activate warp drive." Ed sounded tense, and David realized how nervous he himself felt. None of them understood exactly how it worked. Einstein had explained the controls to Grace, but he hadn't given many details about the fundamentals. Not that there was much to control. It could be turned on or off, and the acceleration could be varied slightly; that was basically it. David flipped through the modes on his monitor until he was looking at the navigation data.

"Here goes," Grace said. "Turning on." Her fingers hesitated a moment above the console, then she pushed the glowing field. "Warp drive active!"

David realized he had been holding his breath as he gulped for air. Nothing happened. He hadn't been pushed against his seat, but remained weightless. There was no noise and the same unmoving stars could be seen through the window. Had something gone wrong? Then his gaze fell on the outboard camera feed. The asteroid was gone.

"Holy shit!" Ed whistled. "If these numbers are right, we're already three billion miles from where we started. That's almost the distance from Earth to Pluto. In less than sixty seconds!"

"And still, at this speed you would need one and a half months from Earth to Alpha Centauri," Einstein added. "And much, much longer to reach the limits of the universe. Luckily, our speed and acceleration will continue to increase."

"You can say that again," Grace said, "the numbers are flying across my monitor. I'm going to have to change to light-years to even read them."

"I'd expected some kind of optical effect," David said. "Doesn't the artificial gravitational field bend the light?"

"Yes," Einstein answered. "But the effect is still minuscule. It will increase as we become faster."

"There should be a blue shift, right?" Grace asked.

"No." Einstein shook his head. "Remember, space is moving with our ship in it, the Magellan is not moving in space. Since we are not traveling with a relative speed, there can be no relative effects."

The sun of the solar system they'd just left fell first slowly, and then quickly, away. Soon, it was just one star among many.

"We've been traveling twelve minutes," Wendy whispered. "And we've already gone one light-year. Unbelievable."

Gradually, more stars outside their windows changed position and fell behind them.

"Imagine if humans had developed warp drive," Ed said, staring out in thought. "We could have conquered the Milky Way."

They all stayed in the bridge, watching the stars glide sublimely beyond the large window.

Chapter 14

"Anybody want some of mine?" Ed asked. Two bites had been more than enough for him. Some of their meals, all pre-packed on trays that just needed to be taken out of the shelf and reheated, tasted pretty good. The steaks in particular were much better than you'd expect for freeze-dried and rehydrated food. But the fish was disgusting. One bite of the pasta with salmon sauce and he'd had enough. Though he had to admit, it did taste just like the grub made by the NASA cooks in Houston—he had to keep reminding himself that it had somehow been synthesized by the AI on the asteroid.

"No thanks," Wendy answered. David and Grace ignored him. His colleagues didn't seem to have much appetite either, all of them picked at their food without enthusiasm.

"Where's Einstein by the way?" Ed asked. Some time ago he'd unstrapped himself and floated to the back.

"I think he's in his module," David answered.

"His module?" Ed asked. "Since when does the sensor module belong to him alone?"

David shrugged. "I was working in my lab and he came in, said hi, and floated past me. He turned right at the node, so I guess he must be in his sensor module."

The module that had been added to their ship along with the warp drive was a small pressurized space with equipment and instruments mounted to the wall. Einstein had showed it to the crew on their first tour of the space-ship. There had been no mention of him wanting it for his own private chamber. Ed had wanted to store things there, but the physicist had insisted it be kept the way it was.

"What's he doing in there?" Ed asked. "There's hardly room to turn around!"

David shrugged again. "Doesn't matter to me. He's not bothering anyone."

Ed grunted and undid the belt that kept him from floating away during meals. He took his tablet and pushed it into the waste container. Even if he went hungry that night, he wasn't going to eat any more of that fish. He went to a console on the wall and turned on the monitor, which immediately filled with white numbers against a black background. He studied the navigation data, sent from the main computer on the bridge. It was hard to digest the meaning of the numbers. "Fifty thousand light-years in just under five hours. And our speed is still increasing exponentially."

"Show us the outboard camera," Grace requested.

Ed flipped a switch.

"Wow! That looks like something out of *Star Trek*!" David exclaimed. "The stars are whizzing by!"

"How fast are we going?" Wendy asked.

Ed looked back at the first monitor. "Hundred and fifty light-years per minute."

"At that speed, we could reach Alpha Centauri from Earth in two seconds," David calculated. "What's really unbelievable is that there's no limit to how fast we can go. We just keep getting faster."

"I still can't believe that we're circling the entire universe," Wendy said.

"I try not to think about it," Ed replied.

"What's the plan now, exactly?" Wendy asked. "We left so quickly, I kind of lost track."

"No wonder," Ed answered. "If there even is a plan. If you ask me, they just threw us in here, set a course, and said: Off you go."

"Well there is some benchmark data," David said. "I've calculated from the flight data that we should reach the edge of the observable universe, forty-five billion light-years away, in about thirty days. Then we'll know whether there's anything behind it to account for Dark Flow."

"And then?" Ed asked. That was not, after all, the end of their mission, but only their secondary goal.

David shrugged. "Then we'll see. Maybe we'll be able to calculate the curvature of the universe from there and can figure out how long we'll need to get all the way around."

Ed had a funny feeling it wasn't going to be that easy. "Yeah, we'll see."

Chapter 15

"Oh my God!" David exclaimed, rubbing the sleep from his eyes. He'd expected something like this, but the view from the bridge windows took his breath away.

"There are no more stars," Grace murmured. "Just blurry lights."

"It's mind-blowing," Ed agreed.

"We've only been flying sixteen hours, and already we've left the galaxy," Grace said.

"We haven't just left it," David explained. "It's already far behind us. We've gone half a million light-years!" He pushed off Ed's seat and floated slowly backward to his own spot, taking care not to hit Einstein with his foot. David strapped himself in and activated his console. The monitor lit up and he switched to the navigation sensors. The data came from the module Einstein had retreated to the night before. David's speculation was confirmed. They were in an intergalactic void. The next galaxy was four hundred thousand light-years away. They wouldn't even pass its tail.

"I'll turn the ship around," Ed said. "Maybe then we

can see the galaxy we launched from." He reached for the control stick.

"I thought we couldn't change our direction of flight during warp drive," Wendy said.

"We can't," Grace answered for Ed. "But we can maneuver within the bubble."

"Rotation, yes," Einstein added. "But no translational movements please."

Ed pushed the control stick to the left without commenting. David couldn't see the movement, since there were no stars, but he could feel it. After a while, a hazy patch of light appeared in the window and Ed stopped the rotation.

"That must be it," he said. "A spiral galaxy, a lot like the Milky Way."

"Not exactly," Einstein said. "Going by the Hubble sequence, we would classify this galaxy as type SBm. It's smaller and slightly irregular, similar to the Large Magellanic Cloud."

"Wise guy," Ed muttered.

"It's like you can watch it getting smaller," Wendy whispered.

"You probably can," David answered. "We're flying faster by the second."

"Where's the Milky Way?" Wendy asked.

Einstein furrowed his brow and stared out the window. Finally he pointed. "There. Far behind the nameless galaxy we started from, around twenty degrees to the left."

"So we can't see it from here," Wendy stated.

"No," Einstein confirmed. "If we could, we'd see it as it looked eighty-one million years ago, but its stars were already encased in spheres by then."

"When were the spheres around the suns in the Milky Way built?" David asked.

"Five billion years ago."

"So once we've flown five billion light-years," Ed interjected, "we'll be able to turn around and look at the Milky Way with our telescopes?"

"Theoretically," David answered. "If the telescopes were strong enough. But back then the Milky Way probably looked nothing like what we're used to."

"So we'd have a hard time finding the sun?"

"We couldn't find it," David answered.

"And why not?"

"First, because the Milky Way has so many stars. Up to three hundred billion. It'd be like trying to find a grain of sand on the beach from an airplane."

"And second?" Ed asked.

"Second, our sun didn't exist five billion years ago. It's only four and a half billion years old."

Ed was silent.

"So what we see is the area the aliens blotted out with their spheres."

"Yes," David answered, even though the question had been directed at Einstein.

"Then why are there so many galaxies?"

"They're behind the area the aliens covered."

"So how big is the area your friends have taken by now?" Ed asked Einstein.

He shrugged. "It's shaped roughly like a sphere with a diameter of one hundred and seventy million light-years."

"Are you saying we're looking at galaxies that are more than one hundred and seventy light-years away?"

Einstein shook his head. "No, you can't see that far with the naked eye. David's conjecture was wrong. What we're looking at are dwarf galaxies in front of the spheres. The galaxy that we left last night was part of a large, local cluster with numerous satellites. Perception can be deceptive."

David nodded. He'd already noticed that some of the blobs of light had moved over the past few minutes. He couldn't have seen that if they were almost two hundred million light-years away. It made sense. Even their own Milky Way had dozens, if not hundreds, of dwarf galaxies that were sometimes only a couple of thousands of light-years across.

"Are we still in the Local Group?" Grace asked.

"What's the Local Group?" Ed asked.

"The cluster of galaxies closest to the Milky Way," David explained. "Andromeda, the closest large galaxy, is also part of it. But the Local Group has a diameter of about eight million light-years. We're far away from it already. My guess is that we're in the Virgo supercluster, which connects some of the nearest galaxy clusters to the Milky Way."

"Correct," Einstein confirmed. "Albeit already at its margins."

"Cluster, supercluster … I never really understood all those structures," Ed said, flipping through the modes of his monitors.

"It's not that complicated," David answered. "To a certain degree it's a random categorization. More interesting is when we first see the large-scale structure of the universe."

"How's that?"

"Looking at the known galaxies, if you zoom way out, a clear structure emerges. It looks kind of like a bubble bath, with smaller and larger bubbles. All of the matter in the universe is at the walls of those bubbles, which are all interconnected. They're also called filaments."

"And what's inside the bubbles?" Ed asked.

"Nothing."

"What do you mean 'nothing'?"

"Alright, maybe not *nothing*, but there are a lot less galaxies in the empty spaces than you'd expect. We call them voids. They can be millions of light-years across. In the course of time, they'll become emptier and emptier, since their mass is pulled toward the gravity of the walls."

"Except time's run out," Grace said.

David pressed his lips together. He'd forgotten. In a few years, it would all be gone. No more galaxies, no clusters, no superclusters, no voids. Nothing. All vanished!

"Still, how those structures appeared in space is an interesting question," Wendy said. "Assuming that matter was distributed evenly after the Big Bang, how were the bubbles formed?"

"There aren't any conclusive answers," David replied. "There are speculations of course. Some scientists think it's the result of quantum effects during the inflationary phase right after the Big Bang. Others think it was caused by Dark Matter." He shot Einstein a questioning look.

"No," he answered. "We have no new knowledge."

"And if you zoom out even further?" Ed asked.

"Then it looks homogenous again," David said. "Imagine you're looking at the foam on the waves of a stormy sea."

"OK."

"If you're swimming in the water, you can see each individual bubble with the galaxies all in a row along the edge. But if you're in a plane, you see only the larger waves, not the bubbles." David paused to give his words time to sink in. "And if you look from outer space, it's all one blue plane from horizon to horizon. No bubbles, no waves."

"So there are no larger structures?"

David lifted his hands. "At least none that we've found."

Einstein cleared his throat. "Who knows? Maybe there are large structures, just no one has discovered them yet." He grinned at David. "Maybe the universes even exhibit a certain structure in the web of reality."

It sounded like pure conjecture, but the words gave David goose bumps.

Chapter 16

David activated the telescope with the lowest magnification and set it to automatically sweep the sky. The computer created a three-dimensional map from the results on the largest monitor on David's console. Right now they were flying in a large void between enormous filaments. The void was two hundred million light-years long. At their current speed, they would cross it within hours. Since leaving fourteen days ago, they had put more than four billion light-years behind them, or ten percent of the distance to the edge of the visible universe. And their ship was still accelerating.

David pointed another telescope in the direction of their tail and pulled its image up. It covered maybe half of one degree, or about the diameter of the moon as seen from Earth. It was filled with stars.

No, David reminded himself. Those weren't stars, they were galaxies. In this small segment of the sky alone were thousands of galaxies, each containing billions and billions of stars. He couldn't say which one they'd come from. Einstein was right. If the minuscule wormhole let them down, they'd never find their way back. Of course, David had always known how big the universe was, he was an astrophysicist after all. But knowing something and experiencing it with your own body by flying across it were two completely different things. He took some pictures and turned back to the monitor with the three-dimensional map. The numbers at the margin had stopped. Looks like the computer had frozen again. That had happened regularly onboard the Helios. David pressed a button and the monitor flickered and reset. The nearest galaxy cluster had come quite a bit closer. Even light would have needed millions of years for the distance that they'd just crossed in under an hour. David was just about to turn on the spectrometer when he heard Ed's voice from their living quarters. The hatch to the module was closed, so he must be screaming. David could just make out the word "asshole." He thought he'd better take a look.

David turned off the monitors, but left the sensors running. He could examine the recordings later. He undid his seatbelt and pushed himself off from his console, floating quickly toward the door of his lab. Using a handhold, he pulled himself through the short connecting tunnel and opened the door to their living quarters. Inside, he found Ed and Einstein. Ed's face was twisted in rage, while Einstein looked completely innocent.

"I don't believe a word of it, you goddamn liar," Ed screamed.

"There is no other answer I can give," Einstein replied calmly.

David approached them, preparing to hold back Ed, who looked like he was about to physically attack the scientist. "What's going on?" he asked.

"He's lying through his teeth," Ed yelled, jabbing a

finger at Einstein's chest. The movement pushed the scientist against the kitchen wall.

"I am not!" he answered.

Like they were two toddlers fighting over a toy!

David turned to Ed. "And what is he supposedly lying about?"

"Everything!" Ed was no longer screaming, but his voice still hurt David's ears.

"Can you give an example?"

"I asked him again how long the trip will take."

"And?"

"And he said he figures three to four months."

"And …?"

"I remember exactly that he said two to two and a half months at our first meeting."

David couldn't remember. He turned to Einstein, who was shaking his head.

He adjusted his plaid jacket with both hands. "That was going by the premise that the diameter of the entire universe was ninety billion light-years. It was simply an example for the scale of magnitude we are dealing with."

"There's a huge difference between two and four months! At NASA we always knew exactly how long a mission would last and how far we needed to fly. Imagine Neil Armstrong had taken off without knowing whether the moon orbits close to Earth or at the edge of the solar system. If it had been the latter, they never would have gotten there."

"You can't compare the two," David said. "Our first destination is the foundation for the second."

"Oh, really?"

David nodded. "At the edge of the observable universe we can take measurements that, together with the wormhole parameters, will allow us to determine the curvature of the universe. Once we know that, we'll know exactly how far we have left to go."

"Yeah, that plan worked great with the lost probes."

In his peripheral vision, David saw Grace and Wendy floating in from the bridge. "What's going on?" Wendy asked.

David ignored her and kept Ed in his sight. "We just have to be careful."

Ed laughed out loud. "We were careful at the edge of the solar system, too. Didn't do us much good. I don't even want to know what's waiting for us this time. God maybe? Ready to send us straight to hell for our hubris?"

"Don't be such a drama queen," Wendy said.

"You know what?" Ed turned his head and gave Einstein an ice-cold stare. "I can't shake the feeling that the aliens are lying to us through their teeth. No matter how innocent this Nobel Prize winner tries to look." He moved to jab Einstein again, who swiftly dodged Ed's finger. David was surprised that the physicist remained so calm.

"I did not lie to you," he replied.

Ed crossed his arms. "Maybe you didn't," he said coolly. "But you sure didn't tell us everything you know."

"That is pure speculation."

Ed snorted and turned around.

"Where are you going?" Wendy asked.

"Out of here. I don't want to see his face anymore. I'm going to the bridge. If you want to do us all a favor, make sure he doesn't follow me."

Chapter 17

"Hi, how's it going?"

David turned around to see Grace float into the lab. She reached for a handheld and deftly changed direction, slowing herself in mid-flight. With the other hand, she reached for the edge of his console. She turned and stopped next to his workstation. "What are you doing?"

"Monitoring our environment," he said, looking back at the display.

Grace came closer until her face was right next to his. He could feel her warmth on his cheek.

She giggled. "You're looking at galaxy clusters. Kind of funny to call them 'our environment.'"

He turned towards her and smiled back. "At the speed we're going, you could even say our local environment— we won't be here long."

He changed the display. A white line crossed the monitor from right to left. It went through what looked like a white mass of clouds against a dark background. "That's our trajectory from the past twenty-four hours. We've gone almost three billion light-years. At that scale, structures disappear and galaxy clusters, filaments, and voids are nothing but minuscule details. We must have passed millions of galaxies since yesterday."

"Each with billions of stars," Grace added. She sounded thoughtful rather than cheerful now.

"At least the big ones like our Milky Way."

"Theoretically, every single one of those solar systems could be home to intelligent civilizations."

"Very theoretically," David answered. "In reality, it's sure to be a lot less. From what Q told us, it's no more than four or five per galaxy."

"Of which there are still billions in the universe."

"Even more. Assuming there are at least a trillion galaxies, there must be so many extraterrestrials that we can't even grasp the number." He pulled up a small calculator on his monitor. "If there were only one civilization in each galaxy in the universe and we wanted to get to know them all … If we visited one each hour and only talked with the aliens for a short time, then we would be …" He entered some numbers into his keyboard. "We would be traveling for more than one hundred million years."

They were silent as they contemplated the length of the number on the monitor.

After some minutes, it was Grace who broke the silence. "One week left until we reach the edge of the universe."

David nodded. "Yeah, we've already gone more than sixty percent of the distance. More than twenty-six billion light-years."

"Sixty percent?" Grace asked. "Shouldn't we start braking?"

David shook his head. "We're not going to brake."

Grace's eyes widened. "We're not?"

"Nope," David answered. "I spoke with Einstein and Ed, we'll take the measurements we need during flight."

"And Ed was OK with that?"

David nodded. "He was glad. If we don't brake and continue at this speed, we can cover more ground in the same time and save on stores."

"But we have enough for months. Hopefully we won't be traveling that long."

David shrugged. "I hope so, too. Another week, then we'll know."

"What do you think?"

David opened his mouth to answer, then closed it. Fact of the matter was, he had no idea. Einstein seemed convinced that the universe had a diameter of a couple of hundred billion light-years at most, but David—like Ed—couldn't shake the feeling that they weren't being told the whole truth.

"David?"

He turned his head to look Grace in the eyes. He couldn't say why, but suddenly, he felt a compulsion to touch her. Embarrassed, he quickly turned back to the computer. "Sorry. I was thinking about Einstein," he said quietly.

"It is uncanny," Grace answered. "Like, is there anything of the real Einstein inside him?"

David had frequently asked himself the same question in the past few weeks. But he didn't have an answer. Einstein seemed like a real person—he looked like one, he acted like one, he even smelled like one. It was definitely easier for David to deal with him day to day if he just believed he *was* a real person.

"What will we see out there?" Grace changed the subject, since David still wasn't saying anything.

"It's one of humanity's most profound questions: What is beyond the horizon of our universe?"

"What do you think?"

David had to grin. "Easy: More universe."

Grace raised her eyebrows. "You mean we'll look out and not see any difference?"

"Exactly. Principle of equality. Why should it look any different somewhere else in space than it does here?"

Grace scratched her chin. "But you yourself were talking about the structure of space with its galaxy clusters and voids. So it's not the same everywhere."

"True. But that all disappears when you increase the scale."

"There could even be larger structures. I mean, larger than the observable universe."

David put his head to one side. He had to think about what Einstein had said recently. He'd taken some cosmology seminars and even sat in on a guest lecture by Alan Guth, who had come up with the inflation theory. But he'd never gone into it in depth, and David knew nothing about the newest developments. All he knew was that many theories had never been proven, even the ones accepted by most of the scientific community. Including the inflation theory—and of course string theory, which had many opponents.

"The truth? I have no idea," David admitted. "But we'll see. We'll be the first people to find out what's behind our universe. I know more than one physicist who would give their life for that privilege."

"But not you?"

David thought about it. Of course you had to take risks to make new discoveries. Certainly he'd taken one when he'd agreed to the Helios expedition. But this? This he'd have rather left to someone else. The only reason he was here was because he had no choice. "Not me," he answered curtly.

Grace grinned at him. She reached out her hand and stroked his shoulder. "You've changed a lot," she said, a warmth in her voice that made David nervous. He almost blushed.

"You think so?"

Grace nodded. Her hand was still on his shoulder, which was burning like fire despite the fabric between her skin and his. "First time I met you in Houston, you were a shy, scared little boy. I remember I almost laughed out loud when I heard you were going to be one of the participants on the mission to the margins of the solar system. But the training and the flight have changed you. You've become a man. You faced your fears, you even confronted Ed. I know experienced astronauts who wouldn't dare to do that."

"Thanks," David croaked. "But what are you trying to tell me?"

Finally, she drew back her hand. "Nothing." She grinned at him and her stare gave him goose bumps. "Nothing at all." Turning around, she pushed off the seat and floated toward their living quarters.

Chapter 18

"Hi Ed. Everything OK?"

Ed jumped at the sound of Wendy's voice. He hadn't heard her come in, but of course he hadn't closed the door and there were no footsteps in zero G. He turned around and smiled at her. "Of course, Everything A-OK."

"Feel like company?"

Ed hesitated. He enjoyed these peaceful moments, surrounded only by the instruments that gave him control over the spaceship. On the other hand, he'd been sitting there almost two hours and he didn't want to fall asleep. Not that the spaceship actually needed him. Finally, he nodded. "Sure." He gestured to the pilot's seat next to him, normally Grace's spot.

Wendy grabbed a handheld above her, turned elegantly around, and pushed herself feet first toward the seat. Once in, she fastened the seatbelt so she could move without floating away and craned her head to see out the bridge window. "It's so dark outside."

"Give your eyes some time to get used to it," Ed said.

They sat in silence, while Ed flipped through displays on his console before settling on the navigation data.

"Now I'm slowly starting to see something," Wendy said quietly. "Those flecks of light zipping by … Can those be galaxies?"

Ed nodded. "Yup. Those are the galaxies. Like passing a cloud of mosquitos on the highway. I almost expect them to hit the windows any second."

"Turn on your wipers," Wendy quipped. "How fast are we going?"

Ed looked at the monitor. "Almost fifty thousand light-years per second." He whistled softly. "We'd be across the Milky Way in two seconds."

"And hit Andromeda in under a minute," Wendy added.

"If the numbers are right, it's only two more days before we reach the end of the universe," Ed said.

"The *observable* universe," Wendy reminded him. "I wonder what lies beyond it."

Ed just shrugged his shoulders. He had to think again about the probes that Einstein and the aliens had lost contact with. If there was some kind of obstruction or some other danger, they'd never even notice it at the speed they were going. "Maybe God's put up a construction fence to secure the end of the world."

"Spare me your sarcasm," Wendy said. "I'm scared enough as it is."

Ed's laugh came out more like a bark. "Scared of dying?"

"Yes!" Wendy said so loudly that Ed jumped. "I'm scared of dying," she added more softly.

Ed shrugged his shoulders. He couldn't say the same for himself. As far as he was concerned, there were two possibilities. Either there was life after death, as his religion

—which he'd always taken seriously—claimed, and he would face the Last Judgment, where he was sure to pay for how egoistic he'd been in life. Or there was nothing. Over and out. Neither option was particularly attractive, but everyone had to face it sooner or later. He'd long since come to terms with that. "We'll find out," he said.

"Imagine if Anderson could see you now," Wendy suddenly said.

Ed turned his head to look at her. Wendy gave a wan smile.

Roger Anderson! He'd been Ed's biggest rival in the NASA astronaut corps. Ed didn't want to think about that jerk.

"Anderson is dead," he said.

After a pause, he had to suddenly grin. "But he must be turning over in his grave that I'm the one who got this mission."

"What did he always call you? Angel? I never got that."

Ed made a face. "Not Angel, Engle. After Joe Engle. He was supposed to be the pilot on the Apollo 17 flight, but after the geologists put pressure on Congress, he was traded for Harrison Schmitt. Anderson and I both wrongly thought we were shoe-ins for the moon mission." Ed took a deep breath. "He had a new nickname for me after the ISS collision with the Progress, when we had to jump ship."

"Do tell."

Ed sighed. "Captain Crunch."

Wendy giggled.

"May he rest in peace," Ed said. He couldn't stop himself from smiling, though. Anderson really would be turning over in his grave. "Circling the universe ..."

"What?"

"Just thinking aloud."

"It's an insane mission, isn't it?" Wendy said. There was no emotion in her voice.

Ed shrugged his shoulders. "Crazy to think that we just fly off in one direction and at some point end up back where we started. Can the universe really be curved in on itself? It sounds completely implausible."

"David's a physicist and he thinks space is curved."

It was true, the kid was smarter than he was. Plus he'd already proved aboard the Helios that he could think outside the box. Ed was a dimwit compared to him. If David thought it was theoretically possible, what choice did he have but to believe him? On the other hand … "I always thought the universe was infinite," he said quietly.

"And I've read that ours might not be the only universe," Wendy replied.

Ed clicked his tongue. "To tell you the truth, it's all over my head. I don't even know what the difference is exactly between 'universe' and 'observable universe'."

"That's probably because scientists use the same word to mean different things," Wendy said. "David explained it to me the other day. Astronomers mean what they can see through telescopes. For them, everything else belongs to a parallel universe. Cosmologists turn up their noses at that idea. For them, 'universe' means all of space. Whether or not you can see it from Earth. Either way, there's no separation between our part of outer space and regions beyond our cosmic horizon. But when cosmologists talk about parallel universes, they mean universes that actually exist apart from ours, that we can't reach."

"And where are they supposed to be?"

Wendy shrugged. "Don't ask me. Try David. Or better yet, Einstein and the aliens."

Ed said nothing for a moment. "I still think they're

trying to pull the wool over our eyes. I'm sure they've got some ulterior motive."

"Such as?"

"I don't have a clue. But I bet you we'll find out soon." He looked at the monitor in front of him. "Maybe even the day after tomorrow, when we hit the edge of the universe."

"The edge of the observable universe."

Ed shrugged again. "Whatever."

Chapter 19

"Can you come over and help me out here?" Grace's tinny voice asked over the intercom loudspeakers.

David leaned over to the microphone in the wall and pressed the talk button. "Sure, on my way. Just give me a minute." He let go of the button and, feet in the holds, pulled himself back down into a sitting position. He would have liked to stay until the telescope was done with its observations, but he could leave it on automatic and check the results later. He made sure the programming was correct and turned off the monitor. Sighing, he pulled his feet out of the straps under the seat and pushed himself off the console, so that he was floating at the center of the laboratory module. Gripping a plastic strap on the ceiling, he pulled himself to the back exit of the module.

Grace had gone by more than an hour earlier. She'd smiled and winked at him and passed through the rear hatch. David wondered once more whether she was flirting with him or just wanted to deepen their work friendship. He'd had too little experience with women to figure it out. His only halfway romantic contact with the opposite sex had been a drunken kiss shared with another student at a college party. Not counting the two rejections he'd suffered when he'd misinterpreted friendliness as interest in a relationship. The first time, he'd gotten himself slapped; the second time, he'd been laughed at humiliatingly. After that, he'd decided the whole thing was too complicated and he should just stick to quantum field theory.

And now here he was—here, of all places—stuck in another such situation. The best strategy was probably just to ignore Grace's strange behavior. On the other hand, he had to admit that she was a fascinating woman. And good-looking. Her short brown hair framed her prominent cheekbones and Grecian nose. He knew Grace was a lesbian; he'd met her former partner on Earth. Which made it even more difficult to gauge her behavior. Of course she could be bisexual, he didn't know about that. But he had caught himself more than once in the past few days staring at her lips and wondering what it would be like to kiss her.

Once again, David felt warmth spreading from between his legs and he forced himself to think about something else. He floated past the connecting mode that led to the warp drive and Einstein's sensor module. The hatch was closed, but David knew that Einstein was in the tiny room. It was where the Nobel Prize winner spent most of his time, and David wondered what he actually did in there. He thought about paying him a short visit, but decided against it and continued on to the engine module.

Grace floated near where the cylindrical Penning trap that held the antimatter rested in its nook. David forced himself to smile and hoped it would keep Grace from noticing how nervous he was. "Hi Grace, how's it going? What's up?" *Did he sound like he was trying to act cool?*

She grinned at him. "Not much, just a small problem I

need your help with. Hope I didn't interrupt anything important?"

He floated toward her and stopped himself on a hand-hold right before the wall. "No, no. I was just checking some measurements, but I can do it later. What can I do for you?"

"I was monitoring the storage cylinders and saw one of the holders is jammed. Probably just blocked by a magnet."

"So what should I do?"

"Hold the cylinder, while I reset the magnets in the duct."

"No prob." He took the cylinder's handles from her. Their fingers touched and he felt a small electrical shock. He must be statically charged. Grace had obviously felt it too, since she giggled softly. David tried not to blush, but he was pretty sure his efforts were in vain.

Grace patted his back almost tenderly, making him even more nervous. She pushed off the floor to a console on the opposite wall. "At my signal, push the cylinder forcefully into the hole. You'll feel a slight resistance to the thrust from the magnet, but with enough momentum you can get it in."

David gulped at Grace's words. Was that a sexual innuendo? Didn't her words have a slight undertone? What could he answer? Something equivocal that showed he was interested without seeming too eager. "OK," he said tonelessly.

"Now!" Grace flipped a silvery lever. David held the magnet trap and pushed it down until it slowly sunk into the hole. The resistance was quickly overcome and the cylinder disappeared into the recess. A green light lit up on the top of the storage cylinder.

"Perfect," Grace said, and clapped her hands. "It really was the magnet switch. We're done."

Unsure what to do next, David floated in front of the wall.

"Come over here," Grace ordered.

David looked up. She was sitting in front of her console with that suggestive expression on her face. Her lips were shining in the light of the module. He pushed off and floated slowly over to the stool next to Grace. Lowering himself, he stared into her eyes. His pulse was racing.

Grace bent toward him. "I have another task for you," she whispered, her mouth close to his ear. She pulled her head back and grinned at him conspiratorially.

She wants to seduce me. It was an absurd factual analysis of the situation, but there was no other possible interpretation. Was he going to let it happen? You bet he was.

David could feel his pants getting tighter. He was going to have to take the initiative, or he'd look like a wimp. "I know what you want from me," he said, with all the confidence he could muster.

She turned her head to the side and grinned even more. "And, what do I want?" she asked, feigning innocence.

Now or never.

He leaned forward and reached for her head with his right hand. He closed his eyes and put his lips on hers.

Grace jerked her head back. Their lips made a smacking sound as they separated and David opened his eyes in shock. She was staring at him in infinite astonishment, and blushing.

Shit! He'd gauged the situation wrong again. Completely wrong.

Grace started to giggle.

David pulled his feet from the holds under his seat and

floated to the back, his hands in front of his body defensively. "I ... I ... ," he stuttered.

"David ..." she began, but her giggles turned into all-out laughter.

His cheeks were burning. He must be as red as a fire hydrant. "I ... I ..." He was simply unable to form a coherent sentence. "I ... I'm sorry,"

Finally, Grace got control of herself. She wiped her mouth with her arm and grinned at him. "I'm afraid you've misunderstood me," she said, and started laughing again.

If there had been gravity on board the spaceship, David would have sunk into the floor. As it was, he had to remain floating, a bundle of embarrassment at the center of the propulsion module. Couldn't one of the antimatter storage cylinders just explode and save him? "I ... thought, I ..." he gasped for breath.

Grace shook her head. At least she wasn't mad at him. Not that laughing at him was much better. "Maybe it was my fault, too," she said. "I wanted to play a joke on the others, lighten things up—see if we couldn't fool them at dinner tonight."

How humiliating! This would now be between them until the end of time. She would never take him seriously again! What had he done?

"I'm sorry," David muttered again, pushing himself off the wall and into the tunnel to the connecting node. He wanted to get as much distance between the two of them as possible before he started to cry.

Chapter 20

"Twenty seconds," said Grace. She took a quick look out the bridge windows and then lowered her head again to view her console. She had begun the countdown ten minutes earlier and had been announcing the time ever since. It was driving Ed crazy—they all had the numbers on their monitors already.

"Ten seconds," Grace announced. Ed opened his mouth to make a sarcastic comment, but held himself in check in the last second. He stared silently at his monitor.

"Five ... four ... three ... two ... one ... now!"

Ed had a hard time feeling excited. The moment was too abstract, and it wasn't like it had any concrete effect on their flight. There was just one thing Ed was interested in. "David?"

"Yes, confirmed. We've gone exactly forty-five billion light-years. We have reached our first destination."

"Can you believe it?" Grace asked. It was obvious from her voice that she didn't. "We're at the edge of the universe."

"The edge of the observable universe as seen from

Earth," Einstein corrected. He was back in his seat next to David. Ed had barely seen him the past couple of days. Not that Ed had missed him, but he would like to know what he did in that tiny module all day.

"I have something for you," the Nobel Prize winner said. "Ed?"

Ed turned around. Einstein held up a bag filled with a yellow liquid. Ed took it and looked at it skeptically. "What is it?"

"Champagne," Einstein answered, pushing a second bag in Grace's direction. She grabbed it as soon as it had floated close enough. "Champagne?" she echoed in amazement.

"Exactly. I thought we should celebrate this moment in style." Einstein also gave a bag to David and to Wendy and pulled a final one for himself out of the rucksack he had attached to his seat.

Ed shrugged, pulled the tab open and sucked on the straw. The bubbly tasted sweet and flat. But of course Einstein knew that carbonation would give them gas in zero G.

"I have something to show you," David said. "SharinHold on, I'm sharing a telescope image with your monitors."

A pattern of red and blue dots appeared on Ed's screen. It looked a little like a work by some modern artist who had randomly thrown paint onto canvas. "And what is that supposed to be?"

"That's a look back at where we came from. In the microwave range."

"That's the cosmic microwave background, isn't it?" Grace asked.

"Yes, we took images like this from Earth, too. They're the earliest images of the cosmos that we have. It's the first light of the universe, from about three hundred and eighty thousand years after the Big Bang, when space became opaque."

"And what's so interesting about it?" Ed asked.

"It's also the light that's farthest away from us. An image of the cosmic microwave background is an image of the margins of the visible universe."

"Where we are now," Wendy concluded.

"Exactly," David said. "This image, taken from here, is interesting for two reasons."

"Being?" Ed asked.

"For one, it's no different from the one taken from Earth, even though from here we can see further. That's a clear indication that the cosmos is mostly homogenous and isotropic beyond our horizon as well."

"And second?" Wendy asked.

"The image I sent you is—like I said—a look back. In terms of direction and time. What you're looking at is the area of the cosmos that contains the Milky Way and Earth —shortly after the Big Bang."

Dumbfounded, Ed stared at the screen. He had to admit it was fascinating. Of course, all astronauts needed a more than basic knowledge of astronomy, and he had heard about the CMB. But he wasn't a scientist and he'd never gone into cosmology in more depth. Still, floating here, at the edge of the universe, looking at an image of his homeland shortly after the Big Bang—it did something to him. He suddenly felt like a part of something bigger. Like somehow everything in the universe was connected by space and time. At the same time, he felt tiny. Looking out from the horizon, Ed felt like he was doing something forbidden. Like God did not mean for them to be here and would punish them if they flew any further. "David!" Ed turned around.

"Yes?" David looked up.

OK, we've looked back. But how do we go forward? What do the measurements say? Can we estimate the time we'll need for our return? Do we know what's up with that Dark Flow we're supposed to take a look at?"

David turned back to his monitors. "I'm doing a high-res telescope scan right now. It'll take a couple of hours to get the results. Then we'll see if we have an explanation for Dark Flow. Judging from the initial lower-res scans, I don't see anything any different from our corner of the universe. What's in front of us looks exactly like what's behind us."

"What about the curvature of the universe? Can we finally say something about that?" Wendy asked.

"Einstein?" David passed the question on.

"Yes. The data is on your console."

"What? Where?"

"There should be a new sensor submenu."

"Oh. Yeah, I see it. Hold on a sec, I have to figure this out."

Ed looked over at Einstein, who was bending over David's console and explaining something quietly.

"I still don't get it," David said. "What do these numbers mean, and how are they generated?"

"A positive curvature of space is situated between zero and one. The greater the curvature, the lower the number."

"And right now it's at 0.8," David stated.

"Which is in the range we thought to be realistic," Einstein added.

Ed groaned. Couldn't they hold off on the lingo until no one else was around? And why hadn't Einstein explained the sensors to David before? Ed just wanted to know one thing: "What does that mean for us? How far do we still have to go?"

Einstein looked at him and smiled. "Again we see that our commander is a man of action—understandable in our current situation."

"Cut the crap, please." Ed had to force himself not to raise his voice. "What's the story?"

Einstein raised his hand. "Let us all remain calm. From this number, we can extrapolate that the universe has a circumference of about two hundred and twenty-five billion light-years, which means we've completed twenty percent of our journey."

Finally! Ed was surprised. He'd expected them to run into problems as soon as they hit the cosmic horizon. Like they had at the edge of the solar system. Instead, it looked like there was nothing special out here—just more galaxies. And they even knew now how far they still had to go. "That means we have to travel one hundred and eighty billion light-years before we're home again. How long will that take us?" He swiveled his head to look at Grace.

"Just finished the calculations. If we keep accelerating until we've gone halfway, then we have another ten days before we begin the braking maneuver—which will last another forty days."

"Fifty days until we're back," Ed said. "I can live with that time frame." He lifted his bag of champagne. "Let's drink to that!"

Chapter 21

"You'd think we'd get some decent food to celebrate," Grace said. "Instead, we have chicken. If this *is* chicken. For some reason, chicken tastes different in space. Tastes like fish, but doesn't look like fish? Must be chicken."

David laughed politely with the others, but as soon as Grace glanced at him, he looked down. He'd been keeping his distance since embarrassing himself—as far as that was possible aboard a spaceship.

"You're right," Ed said. He slapped Einstein on the back, almost causing the scientist to choke. "How come your friends can reconstruct a spaceship atom for atom and build a warp drive that can take us around the universe in two and half months, but they can't make food that tastes better than this?"

"They duplicated the food from the Helios. They assumed you'd chosen it," Einstein answered meekly.

Ed pointed to Einstein's tray. "Honestly. Not even you could like this crap. Don't tell me you think it tastes good?"

Einstein shook his head. "No, it doesn't. But we're not in a Michelin-starred restaurant here."

Ed sighed. "Ain't that the truth."

Wendy had finished her meal and was stowing her tray in its shelf. "Stop talking about good food or I'll start crying," she said, grabbing a bag of apple juice from another shelf before returning to the table. "Did you finish your analysis, David? I mean, the telescope scan."

David nodded. "Yes. I wanted to tell you about it after dinner. We found out what causes Dark Flow."

"Really?" Grace looked up with interest.

David couldn't hold her gaze and turned back to Wendy. "Mmm hmm. I didn't see it at first, but there's a network of galaxy clusters larger than anything we can see in the Hubble volume. At least ten billion light-years across —with a filamentary structure. Its mass must be gigantic, which is why it exerts a gravitational pull on parts of our universe."

"So there are differences?" Ed asked.

David nodded. "Yes. At least in the distribution of mass."

"And I always thought the universe was homogenous beyond the horizon," Wendy said.

"At least we've discovered a phenomenon we never would have found without leaving our corner of the universe."

"Is it relevant for our mission?" Ed asked.

David shook his head. "Relevant? No. But interesting —if you're a physicist."

"How were the differences caused?" Grace asked.

"Must have been slight differences in density when the universe was forming. Probably even happened during inflation."

Ed grunted. "So what is 'inflation' exactly? I've heard the term thrown around a lot, but I have no idea what it really means."

David hesitated. It wasn't an easy concept and he had to think about how to phrase it before speaking. "In the first milliseconds after the Big Bang there was a short phase in which the universe expanded exponentially."

"By how much?" Ed asked.

"An unimaginable amount, even though it took place within a fraction of a second. During this brief phase, the aggregate state of the universe was such that other natural forces could be applied. For example the inflation field, which pushed the universe outwards like dough on speed. Cosmic inflation is also the reason that the universe is so big. Inflation ended with a transitionary phase out of which the universe as we know it was born. Unfortunately, as we now know, it was only metastable, which is why a new transition phase is looming."

"So what's so important about inflation?" Ed asked.

"Well, it helps explain some fundamental astronomical observations."

"Such as?" Wendy asked.

Einstein smiled innocently. David wondered why the Nobel Prize winner didn't participate more in the discussion.

"Remember the image of the cosmic microwave background?"

Wendy nodded.

"It looks the same everywhere. But looking forward and looking back shows us two areas that, according to the old Big Bang theory, were never in contact. So why are they so alike, as if they're in cahoots?" Nobody answered, it was obviously a rhetorical question. "Alan Guth proposed the inflation theory in the late 1970s as a possible answer. In this theory, the two areas of space were once adjacent, they just drifted very far apart in the inflationary phase."

"Isn't his theory widely disputed?" Grace asked. "I remember once reading that."

David laid his head to the side. "True, not all physicists accept the theory, because hardly any of its proposals can be proven. Also, there are some open questions. Many variants on the original theory have been suggested to address these, so there are actually many inflation theories, not one. And of course, some physicists think it's pure speculation."

"Nice to know that physics hasn't solved all of God's open questions."

"My open question is: what do we do next?" Wendy said.

"There are no open questions for us," Einstein answered coldly. He turned, surprised.

"We continue until we have flown around the universe."

"OK by me," Ed said. "At least now we know how long that will take." After a pause, he added: "And when we're back, I want to finally be told what happened to Earth."

Chapter 22

"May I come in?"

Ed started. He must have fallen asleep. His eyes darted to the clock on his console monitor. As usual on a space mission, it had started running at takeoff. MET was now 31:12:38. He couldn't have been sleeping long. Turning around, he waved Grace in. "Of course."

Grace floated in and sat down in her seat. A rarity—not counting the maneuvers where the entire crew was needed at their places. Usually, Grace stayed in the living module—or in the propulsion module, which she was responsible for.

"Anything new?" she asked.

Ed shook his head. "Nope. Same old, same old. Galaxy after galaxy zooming past us in a matter of seconds."

"How fast are we flying now?"

Ed shrugged. "The numeral is so high, I don't even look anymore."

Grace activated her console. "Two hundred million light-years per hour."

"And counting," Ed added.

"Crazy," Grace whispered.

Ed nodded. "Looks like you can toss your antimatter engine."

"I'll wait until we've started the braking phase and are back in the galaxy we started from."

"Hey, at least it shouldn't be too long from now," Ed said.

"If nothing happens."

Ed nodded. "I know, I've got a bad feeling, too. I just can't believe that everything's going to be easy peasy and we just circle the universe in three months. It'd be too good to be true."

"You've been pessimistic from the beginning," Grace reminded him.

"I keep thinking about those lost probes."

"What do you think happened to them?"

Ed sighed. Like he knew. Plenty of crazy ideas battered his brain whenever he had a quiet moment, but not a single one had any substance.

"I haven't the slightest." He sounded more annoyed than he had wanted to. "Maybe some higher alien intelligence has put a sphere around the multiverse." He'd meant it as a joke, but after their last voyage in Earth's solar system, it didn't come out sounding very funny.

"We thought it couldn't get any weirder," Grace said. "But who knows what the universe still holds in store for us?"

"I keep wondering what God thinks about what we're doing. Is it blasphemy? Or could he care less?"

He noticed Grace was giving him side-eye. "You really believe in God? You seem so rational."

Ed laughed out loud. "Don't tell me you really think I'm a rational person?"

Grace nodded. "You threaten to tip the extrovert scale maybe, but yes."

Ed couldn't help grinning. "Maybe you're right." He looked out the window, where a large spiral galaxy was quickly approaching. They sped through its stars and were out again in no time. Ed became serious. "I've always believed in God, though maybe it used to be less important to me. And I still sometimes have doubts. But the older I get, the more I believe in the existence of a creator. I suppose you're an atheist?"

"Yes," Grace answered. "As far as I'm concerned, religion is nothing but a figment of people's imagination. A delusion for those in despair—people desperately trying to give their life meaning, or people who just don't want to accept that death is the end."

"You got any proof for your theory?" Ed asked.

"For God's non-existence?" Grace asked, surprised. "Of course not."

"Then you're just as much of a believer as I am. Only you believe in the religion of the atheists," he said. He'd known plenty of atheists in his time—there had been more than enough of them in the astronauts corps. Some were more rabid missionaries than Christian or Islamic fundamentalists.

"What are you two getting all worked up about?"

Ed turned his head and saw David floating into the bridge. He was carrying a clipboard under his arm.

"We're fighting about who's right," Grace said. "Ed is Catholic and believes in God. I'm an atheist. What do you think?"

David smiled, making sure he didn't look at Grace. "Neither Catholics nor atheists think, they *believe*. If you want to think, you'll have to come join me over by the agnostics."

"What's the difference?" Grace asked.

"As an atheist, you believe that there is no God. As an agnostic, I admit that I don't know, because I have no proof either for or against God's existence."

"So you're keeping out of it?" Ed asked.

"Totally," David answered. "I got out of the habit of discussing the question, it's senseless." David had been holding onto a ceiling handheld, now he pushed himself into his seat. Quickly, he activated the instruments at his console.

"Something wrong?" Ed asked.

David looked up, he seemed unsure what to answer. "Hold on a sec."

Ed's eyes met Grace's. She just shrugged. "If something is wrong, I'd like to know now," Ed said firmly.

David sighed. "I don't know yet. A couple of values seem strange to me, but I need to see whether the console here spits out the same numbers as the one in the lab."

"Values? What kind of values?" Ed asked.

David shrugged. "If the numbers on the console in the laboratory module are correct, then our velocity has increased more than it should."

"Our velocity?" Ed asked. He switched to his own navigation screen. He didn't see anything. They were going steadily faster, but they'd been doing that the whole time. "Can you quantify that?"

David glanced up and looked back at his monitor and keyboard. Ed was about to repeat his question, when David suddenly nodded. "Numbers here are the same."

"So what's with our velocity?"

"It's growing exponentially."

"That's nothing new," Ed said.

"But the acceleration isn't constant, it's also growing."

"Something else we discussed before takeoff," Grace

said and smiled at David, which seemed to make him lose his train of thought.

"Yeah ... um ... but the rate ... I mean the derivative of acceleration up to now ..."

Ed snorted. "Please, no higher algebra! Keep it simple, OK?"

David sighed again. "The acceleration increase has always been linear—up to now, the rate has been constant. Suddenly, it's speeding up."

Ed shot Grace a questioning glance, but she just shrugged again. "Should we be worried?" he asked David.

"I wouldn't go that far, but it's strange that the value has changed."

"By a lot?" Grace asked.

David shook his head. "No," he admitted. "Just enough that I was able to detect it with my instruments."

"Maybe something is wrong with the sensors," Grace hazarded. That was her area of responsibility. "Should we check?"

David shook his head. "No, the numbers come directly from the sensor module that the aliens attached. The data on our position and navigation, which is how our velocity and distance are calculated, come from the wormhole's metrics. The whole system is just a black box for us."

"Looks like it's time to talk to Einstein," Grace said.

David shook his head. "I would wait a bit. It might still be an anomaly."

Ed nodded. "Agreed. But keep an eye on it and make sure I'm kept in the loop."

"Will do." David undid his buckle. "I'm going back to the lab to run a couple more tests." He pushed himself off from a strut and soon disappeared through the hatch to the living quarters.

"Weird," Ed mumbled.

"You worried?" Grace inquired.

"No. At least not yet. But if our acceleration continues to grow, we'd better take a closer look."

Grace gave a short laugh. "You heard him yourself. The sensors are part of the alien module. Just like the propulsion module with the warp drive. It really is a black box. I don't see us taking a closer look at anything."

Ed hadn't liked it from the start that their spaceship was partly made of components they couldn't control. But something else was bothering him, too. "Did David seem a little weird to you?"

"How do you mean?" Grace asked.

Ed could tell from her tone of voice that she knew exactly what he meant, and he suspected that she also knew the reason for David's odd behavior. "Out with it!"

Grace smiled. "I'm afraid David has a bit of a crush on me."

Ed groaned loudly. "Billions of light-years beyond the edge of the world and now this? Doesn't he have any other problems?"

"That's how it is with emotions. Even if we go to the end of the universe, we're still only human."

Emotions! In his opinion, they should have an off button.

Chapter 23

David peeked into the living quarters and breathed a sigh of relief when he saw that only Wendy was there, bending over a laptop. It had been a couple of days, but he still tried to avoid being alone with Grace. Of course she had to pass through his laboratory module on her way to the propulsion module, but in those moments he always made himself very busy. They hadn't discussed the incident again, but whenever she grinned at him when they were together in the group, he was sure she was making fun of him.

He pushed off from a handheld on the hatch and floated into the living quarters. "Hi Wendy."

She looked up from her computer. "Hi David." Her eyes were red and swollen.

"Everything OK?" He stopped himself on the table she was sitting at and strapped himself onto a stool.

Wendy nodded. "I'll be fine."

"What you got there?"

She turned the laptop toward him and he could see a photo of Wendy in the arms of her husband, Gerry.

Behind them was a hazy Japanese pagoda in what looked like a park.

"Isn't it weird?" Wendy asked

"What?"

"They rebuilt the spaceship atom for atom—everything that was on board."

David understood. "Even our personal laptops."

"And all the data on the hard drive. Even our private photos."

He'd noticed that, but since he didn't have any photos or films on his laptop, he hadn't really thought about the significance of the fact. Had the aliens done it on purpose, or had the information just happened to be in the dataset they'd used to rebuild the Helios? They still knew so little about the aliens and their aims. Theoretically, they could ask Einstein, but he was keeping to himself again—and he wouldn't have given a straight answer anyway.

"I shouldn't look at them," Wendy said, and shut her laptop.

David didn't respond. What could he say?

"Gerry is dead. I'll never see him again. I'm only torturing myself by looking at the photos, but I can't stop."

"Maybe you should delete them?" David proposed timidly.

Wendy's opened her eyes wide. "You don't really expect me to do that?"

David realized immediately that he'd said the wrong thing and shook his head.

"Those pictures are all that's left of Gerry and me."

"You could at least put them on a flash drive and lock it up somewhere, so you don't always have them right in front of you."

"Yeah, I could do that maybe." Wendy undid her seatbelt, floated to the lockers, and stowed away her laptop.

"How's your work been going? What about the increase in acceleration? Did it stop?"

David shook his head. He'd been observing the phenomenon for four days now. Secretly, he had hoped it was just an anomaly, or a data artifact, but that hadn't turned out to be the case. "I'm afraid not. On the contrary."

"On the contrary?" Wendy asked. "What do you mean?"

"The increase has become greater and we're going even faster than expected."

"By what percentage?"

David did some quick calculations in his head. "About one percent."

Wendy laughed. "Oh well. It's not like that's very much."

David rubbed his temples. "Maybe not in numbers. But one thing worries me."

"And that is?"

David sighed. "When I first noticed it four days ago, the rate of increase was about one tenth of a percent. Two days ago, it was two tenths."

"What are you trying to say?"

David drew a line in the air with his finger. "If the increases were constant, today we'd have three tenths of one percent, not a whole percent. If you diagram it, you see an exponential increase two days ago."

"Meaning ...?"

"In another four days, we might have a discrepancy of ten percent."

"In four days we'll have gone halfway, and start braking. So we can live with ten percent, can't we?"

In truth of fact, Wendy was right. A ten percent divergence wasn't too much in absolute numbers. "Actually, I was just on my way to the bridge to discuss it with Ed."

Wendy shook her head and waved her hand. "I just came from there. He was asleep in his seat. It's not long until dinner anyway. Why don't you wait until then?"

David said nothing for a moment. Probably Wendy was right. But he still had a bad feeling. He didn't have the slightest idea what was causing the discrepancy—or what it might mean for the rest of their flight. If it was some kind of defect, who knew whether they'd be able to break as planned? "OK. But I definitely want to talk to Einstein. I want to hear what he has to say about it."

"Einstein? I haven't even seen him since our little cele-bration a week ago."

"I know. He grabbed a bunch of dried food and drinks and holed up in his module."

"Six days ago?"

David nodded. "Six days ago."

"Reason enough to find out what he's doing in there," Wendy said, pushing off from the module floor towards the back exit. David followed.

Together they floated quickly through the laboratory and a few seconds later they were in the module that connected to the propulsion module and Einstein's hide-away in the sensor module. On the Orion, the node had led to the capsule in which they'd flown from Earth to the ship, but the aliens hadn't recreated that. It wouldn't have served any purpose on this mission.

Wendy hammered her fists against the hatch. "Ein-stein, are you in there? Come out, we want to talk with you," she called.

"You don't need to shout," David said.

Wendy sighed and reached for the lever that opened

the hatch. She pulled at it, but it didn't budge an inch. "Stuck," she said.

"I bet he blocked the hatch from the inside," David said.

"Why would he do that?" Wendy asked herself out loud. "Why does he isolate himself this way?"

"No idea."

Wendy floated to the back wall of the connecting module and got a tool bag from a net. She took out a large shiny wrench. Then she returned to the door and banged against the metal. David covered his ears while Wendy hammered against the door again and again.

Finally, with sweat on her brow, she gave up. "He definitely heard that. He doesn't want to open up."

"Leave him be. We'll catch him the next time he leaves the module."

David was just about to turn around as the lever moved down and the door opened just enough for Einstein to stick his head out.

"Yes? What is it?" His wavy gray hair stood out in all directions. The reek of tobacco smoke entered David's nostrils.

"Sorry to disturb you," Wendy said, somewhat sarcastically.

"No trouble at all. I was just taking a break."

"A break? What are you doing in there all this time?" David leaned over to one side to catch a glimpse through the crack between door and frame, but Einstein had positioned himself so that nothing could be seen.

"I'm working on a new theory. Maybe I'll be able to reconcile the theory of relativity and quantum physics after all."

David's gaze met Wendy's. He knew exactly what Ed would have said.

"So what is it?" Einstein asked again.

David pointed toward his laboratory. "I've run a few tests and found a deviation in the linear increase of our acceleration."

"And your point is?" Einstein asked.

"Well, it's significant and very clear. We're already one percent above the velocity we should be at, and the rate is increasing."

Einstein waved his hand dismissively. "Slight deviations in warp drive performance are possible, even probable. No cause for concern." He yawned.

David was surprised by Einstein's lack of interest. "Don't you want to at least take a look at the data? I have the impression that it's a systematic effect."

"No, that won't be necessary. No need to worry."

Before David could answer, Einstein had already closed and locked the hatch.

Wendy shrugged. "Well he was a big help. But at least he said we shouldn't worry."

David frowned. His worry level had just risen considerably.

Chapter 24

"Glad to see a certain gentleman is gracing us with his presence," Ed said, as Einstein floated onto the bridge.

David only looked up briefly as Einstein took a seat next to him. He was too engrossed in the sensor data on his console.

"I did not want to miss this special moment," the scientist answered effusively.

"One hundred and twelve billion light-years," Wendy said. "It's hard to fathom."

"The furthest we can get from home," Ed said. "Without even changing our trajectory, we'll soon be heading back to our corner of the universe. Just from the other direction. Do we have green for the braking maneuver?"

"Yes," Grace answered. "We're ready to turn off warp drive, turn the ship, and reactivate the engine. Without changing the mission profile, our velocity will be zero when we're at our starting point."

"At least that's the theory," David mumbled.

"Excuse me?" Ed said.

"Let's just finish the maneuver and evaluate the data before we open any more bubbly," David said. He was pessimistic, although he couldn't say exactly why. Maybe because their velocity had continued to increase more than it should. It was now ten percent above the set value, which was why they were starting to brake three hours earlier than they had originally planned. After ending the maneuver, they would again measure the curvature of the universe. If they had really reached the other end of the universe, their reading should give them a factor of zero point five.

"One more minute," Ed announced.

"Ready over here," Grace said.

"There's one thing I don't get," said Wendy.

"What?" Grace asked.

"When we turn off the warp drive, shouldn't we instantaneously start flying at less than the speed of light?"

"Einstein?" Grace turned around.

He cleared his throat. "Even after turning it off, we're still in a bubble of artificial space-time that is moving through the universe faster than the speed of light. It's as if we've created a wave we are now riding on. It follows its own laws of inertia. We need a counterthrust to reduce the bubble's speed. That's why we turn."

"Which we will do," Ed said with a glance at his monitor, "in exactly ten seconds. On my command in six, five, four, three, two, one, zero!"

Grace pressed override on her console. "Engine off!"

"David?"

"Acceleration had stopped. Speed is constant."

"Glad to hear it!" Ed clapped his hands. "I'll turn the ship manually. Counter-thrust in five minutes."

David's fingers flew across his console. By then, he wanted to have the data on the current curvature. He now knew how to access the information from Einstein's sensor module. Pulling up the screen for the wormhole mouth tension, he obtained the numbers he wanted. Now all the computer needed to do was convert the values and—

David started. The number on the screen couldn't be right. He must have made a mistake. David did the measurements again, and plugged them in again to be calculated.

The value was the same.

David felt his temperature rising and his heart rate going up. "Guys ..." he blurted.

"What's wrong?" Ed asked, turning around.

"We have a problem."

"What?" Ed asked again.

David hesitated. He turned to look at Einstein. "Could you please check the calculation?"

Einstein looked over David's shoulder at his console. "Seems to be correct," he said indifferently.

David swallowed. If that was true, then their situation was far graver than he had feared.

"What's going on?" Ed asked insistently.

David took a deep breath. "The curvature factor should have decreased. Our prognosis, based on the first measurement one week ago, was zero point five."

"Go on!" Ed demanded.

"It's gone up. To almost one."

Ed raised his hands. "Which means ...?"

"An infinite universe!" His voice rose with every word.

"But the value we took a week ago at the edge of the observable universe as seen from Earth ..." Wendy began.

"... must have been a local value, not a global one," David finished. "Imagine you're walking up an upright ring. You're at the bottom and the floor becomes steeper and steeper."

"Go on!" Ed said.

"Well looks like it wasn't a ring, but a hill, since we've gone further, but we're back at the bottom."

"So we won't get home by flying straight," Ed concluded.

David shrugged. "It's still possible that the universe has a three-dimensional curvature, but the radius would have to be trillions or even quadrillions of light-years across."

Ed looked at him a moment in silence and then nodded. "We don't have the stores for a journey that long. Our mission has failed. We'll brake, and turn back."

He turned to look at Einstein. "In the direction we came. Do you agree?"

Einstein shrugged. "Very unfortunate," he said quietly.

"That's all you have to say?" Ed yelled at him, but Einstein did not respond.

"So much for creating a new universe," Wendy whispered. Ed and Grace probably hadn't heard her in their seats in the front. Einstein did not react and David didn't know what to say either. Was she right? Had it all been for nothing? If the aliens really needed a closed topology of the universe to make a new one, then they had indeed failed.

"Isn't there anything we can do?" he asked, turning toward Einstein. He spoke quietly. "A solution that would work even if the universe is infinite?"

Einstein swiveled his head and looked at him. "I don't have any further information on the topic."

The answer irritated David. Not so much what he had said, but how he had said it. "You don't know or you don't want to tell us?"

"Maybe there's something we can do," Einstein mumbled.

"Maybe? Why …?" David glanced at his console,

which had switched back into navigation mode. He'd seen the change in his peripheral vision. But the number on the screen couldn't be right!

"We're going faster again!" He hadn't intended to screech.

Ed and Grace turned to look at him. "What?" they asked at the same time.

"I said we're going faster again."

"That's not possible," Grace explained. "The warp drive is off. You must be wrong!"

"I'm not wrong! We're accelerating—even with the engine off. Einstein?"

He leaned to the side to look at David's console. "Interesting."

"Interesting?" David asked, astonished. He felt himself getting angry. "That's all you have to say?"

"That's all I can say."

What was going on here? David shook his head and changed his console settings. He plugged some numbers into a calculating program and ran some analyses. "Velocity is increasing at ten percent of the original value. It's the exact same exponential component I noticed a week ago."

"How is that possible?" Ed asked. "How the fuck are we accelerating with the engine off? It can't be."

David shrugged, helplessly. "I don't have an answer for you."

Ed leaned back in the commander's chair before turning to Grace. "Retro-thrust. The ship is in retrograde position. We'll brake until our speed is zero. Go!"

Grace nodded and began work at her console. "Ready. I'll start the engine in three, two, one … Engine running." She gasped. "Wait. It's not running. I have a red light."

Ed turned his head. "What happened?"

"The engines are dead," Grace said.

"Einstein!" Ed screamed.

He bent forward slowly. "There's not much I can do," he answered quietly.

"There's not much …" Ed swallowed. "Without the warp drive, we're fucked."

"I'm sorry," Einstein said.

"I'll bet you are," Ed answered. "Dammit all to hell, we'll be speeding through the universe at one thousand times the speed of light for all eternity."

"More than that," David said with a glance at his console.

"More than what?" Ed asked. His face was red.

"Our speed is still increasing exponentially."

"What the fuck difference does it make if it's one thousand or two thousand?" Ed screamed.

"The difference is the exponential growth. Today, we're ten percent faster than we should be," David explained. "In five days, we'll be twice as fast, five days after that, ten times faster and in another week, one hundred times faster. The explosive increase in velocity will just keep on getting larger. Before we know it, we'll be crossing one hundred universes in a split second. Forever. We have to find a way to stop. We have to."

Chapter 25

Ed floated into the laboratory module, Wendy close behind him. David looked up at them briefly and stared back at his computer screen.

"What's up?" Ed asked. He knew it could hardly be something good. Almost four weeks had passed since their failed braking maneuver, and, as David had predicted, they could barely measure their speed. Yesterday alone, they had covered the unimaginable distance of three trillion light-years. That was almost four thousand times the distance from Earth to the edge of the observable universe. Or four thousand Hubbles, as David said. Pretty soon they would be zooming through infinity so quickly, there would be no more units of measurement. Ed sat in his chair in the cockpit for a few minutes, staring out the window. Mostly it was dark. Every once in a while there was a milliseconds-long flare-up when they flew through a particularly dense cluster of galaxies.

David pointed to his monitor. "I wanted to show you something."

"Something bad?" Wendy asked.

David shrugged. "I don't know. But it's interesting."

Ed held on to David's console, bringing himself to a stop. Wendy floated next to him. Ed could see an image from David's telescope on the screen. "What is that?"

"An image of our current position. Edited by the computer so we can get an idea of our environment."

Ed laughed. "Our current position? Our environment? By the time we have that image on the monitor, we'll be Hubbles away."

"It's all we have," David said tersely.

"OK, OK. So what about that picture?"

"It was taken in the direction of flight. Notice anything?"

Ed nodded. It was hard not to see it. "There are no galaxies in the middle. Another void?"

"Look," David said, and pressed a key on his keyboard.

The image changed. The distribution of galaxies was different. The picture must have been taken at another time. But the empty space in the middle was the same. "Hmm. Something wrong with the lenses?"

"No," David answered. "When I rotate the telescope, everything's fine. The phenomenon only appears in the direction of flight and one hundred and eighty degrees opposite. There's one more thing. The galaxies closest to the blind spot are in the red spectrum."

"A redshift?" Wendy asked. "Sounds like an effect of relativity."

David nodded. "I think so, too. My current guess is that it's somehow caused by the warp drive. I even have an idea how. The warp drive curves the space in front of and behind us, in a very small area. It's possible that at very high speeds there are quantum effects and vacuum energy is pumped into the curvature. That would also explain why we're accelerating even though the engine is off."

"But why would the stars—I mean galaxies—disappear in the direction we're headed?"

"Because the artificial curvature of the bubble around us has increased so much, it's formed an event horizon. Similar to a black hole. No light can leave the area, and most of the light that enters from the front is pushed away. The same is true behind us."

Ed took a deep breath. "So what does it mean for us?"

David looked baffled. "I don't know. But if it keeps up, our field of vision will grow smaller and smaller until light only enters from a tiny area at the side."

"What about the light?"

Ed looked up. Einstein had entered the laboratory. He was about to say something caustic, but he bit his tongue.

David pointed to his monitor and the physicist came closer. He listened to David's theories without saying anything. When David had finished, the older man furrowed his brow and began mumbling to himself.

Ed felt himself becoming angry. "What do you have to say about it?" he asked so loudly that Wendy jumped.

"Hmm. An interesting phenomenon. It shows once again that we haven't completely understood warp drive. I think David's conjecture is correct." He turned to look at the young physicist. "You should write a paper on it."

Ed laughed out loud. "A paper? Tell me I didn't hear that right. Who's going to read it?" He chortled and jabbed Einstein's chest. "You know what I think? This is what happened to your probes. Just like our ship, they took on a life of their own and are speeding towards infinity at exponentially growing speeds. But they'll never arrive, since our cosmos is never-ending."

Einstein smiled tentatively. "That is certainly possible."

Ed needed all his self-control not to grab Einstein by

the collar as he floated by. "Where do you think you're going?"

"To get something to eat. I'm hungry," he answered, and disappeared through the hatch to the living module.

Wendy looked at Ed blankly.

"I'm hungry," Ed parroted, then turned to look at David. "Follow him! Keep him in the living quarters with some discussion about science."

"Why?" David asked, dismayed.

"Just do it!" Ed ordered. He gave Wendy a sign to follow him and pushed off toward the connecting module. When he arrived, he let Wendy pass and closed the door to the laboratory.

"You have a plan?" Wendy asked.

"You and I are going to take a look at Einstein's module," Ed said. "I want to know what he's been doing in there all this time."

"You think we'll get in?"

Ed nodded. "The door to the sensor module is the same as all the others. You can close them from the inside, but not from the outside. And you can't lock them at all."

Ed reached for the lever, pushed himself against the floor and pulled with all his might, but it didn't budge.

"Shit, it's really stuck! How the hell does a lightweight like Einstein move it?"

"Maybe the aliens put in some kind of security device to keep us from getting into the module."

Ed snorted. "What's so important about their module that we can't even enter it? It doesn't make sense to get all worked up about a couple of sensors."

He noticed a small hole in the hatch. That was where the Orion capsule had docked aboard the Helios. "Hold on a sec."

Ed pushed off the floor and floated to the ceiling. He

opened a cover and pulled out a tool bag. Rolling it open, he took out an Allen wrench.

"What are you doing?" Wendy asked.

"The Orion capsule had an emergency exit mechanism. Remember? So the divers could get us out of the water even if we were unconscious at reentry."

"And you think that'll work?"

"We'll find out," Ed grunted, and inserted the wrench. He pulled as hard as he could, but the wrench didn't move an inch. "Shit, fuck, piss, hell!"

Ed wiped the sweat from his brow with his right hand, keeping his left hand around the wrench. He searched the module with his eyes. "Can you bring me one of those pipes?"

Wendy pushed herself into the direction Ed had indicated. She returned with a small pipe, meant for the repair of leaky coolant lines. "What do you want with it?"

Ed took the pipe from her and stuck it over the wrench. "Thanks. I need more leverage."

He pulled down on the wrench, bracing his feet on the edge of the hatch. It made a short grinding noise, and the handle moved. Clicking his tongue in satisfaction, he turned the wrench easily. "That's more like it!"

He reached for the lever, which now slid down with no resistance. "I don't know how Einstein locked the hatch, but it didn't help him much," Ed said, opening the door.

He had seen the sensor module once before, when Einstein had given him a tour while they were still inside the asteroid. He hadn't remembered it being so small. Slowly, he floated through the hatch. It smelled like a cross between a smoking lounge and a locker room, even though the ventilation was on. The module was hardly large enough to turn around in. On the right-hand wall was a sleeping bag, where Einstein obviously slept. The other walls were full of an almost grotesque amount of clutter. Photos, pens, notes and books were stuck all over the place with magnets and Velcro. Rumpled clothing could be seen inside a half-open compartment. A half-smoked cigar floated past Ed's chest.

Wendy caught it. "He knows he's not allowed to smoke on board."

Ed just shrugged his shoulders. He'd noticed the smell of tobacco in the connecting node in the very first week. It hadn't bothered him much. His Russian colleagues had also occasionally snuck a cigarette onboard the Mir space station. Ed didn't think it really posed much danger. There were more likely fire sources—that wasn't why he'd broken into the module. He started flipping through the papers on the wall, but all he saw were mathematical formulas. What had he expected? But there had to be something that explained why Einstein always retreated here.

He looked at the wall across from the hatch and noticed that one panel wasn't really closed. Floating over, he pressed the cover, which swung open. Behind it was a computer console with multiple monitors and even more switches. Ed waved to Wendy to take a look. "What do you think of all this?"

"Hmm," his colleague answered. "Looks like the sensor console in David's lab."

Ed nodded. "Yeah, I thought so too, but this one has more switches."

"And they're not all labeled."

"Einstein never told us that he can control the sensors from here too. Why not?"

"No idea. Maybe they're the controls for the wormhole," Wendy suggested.

"The wormhole ..." Ed whistled. "I keep repressing the fact that we've got one of those on board. Not like I could tell you what a submicroscopic wormhole looks like anyway."

"He said it's for data transmission of the sensor measurements to the asteroid mission."

"From this far away?" Ed asked skeptically.

"That's what he said!"

"Do you think he can use it to make contact with the aliens?"

"He claimed it was unidirectional."

"But maybe he's just a goddamn liar." Ed wondered whether he should flip a couple of the switches to see what happened, but that probably wasn't such a good idea.

"We should go," Wendy said.

Ed looked at his watch. Einstein could be back any second. "OK. We won't do anything yet. But more and more I'm starting to think that Einstein has his own agenda."

"You've thought that from the very beginning."

"True. We should keep a closer eye on him. I'll talk to Grace. Maybe she can improvise a surveillance instrument that we can smuggle into the sensor module. I want to know what he's doing in here."

Chapter 26

"You want some of the orange juice?" Wendy asked.

Ed shook his head.

"It's the last one," Wendy added insistently. "Only water left after this."

"Who cares," Ed grunted and made a face.

David couldn't remember the mood on board ever having been this bad. Not even including their flight on the Helios.

To the edge of the solar system.

They'd been so proud of forging so far into space. David glanced over to the navigation data screen that heartlessly confronted them with the current numbers even in the living module. Every second, they were covering a distance twice the circumference of the observable universe as seen from Earth. Their velocity continued to increase exponentially. They had already flown millions of times further than they had originally planned, and they still couldn't make out a global curvature of the universe. They would race toward infinity for all eternity. And their stores had already gotten markedly smaller.

David looked over to Einstein, who was eating with them for the first time in days. He sat lethargically on a stool, his tray strapped to his lap, shoveling mashed potatoes and peas, which tasted as bad as they looked, into his mouth. No one had dared ask him yet. But somebody was going to have to. "Did you find out anything new?"

Einstein stared at him, his fork suspended in mid-air. "What do you mean?"

"The engine. Did you learn anything about how we might repair it?"

Einstein shook his head in what seemed like slow motion. "I'm afraid not, but I'm not quite finished with my analysis."

"What kind of analysis are you running?" Ed asked aggressively. "I thought there were no sensors in the warp drive module. So what do you want to monitor?"

Einstein smiled, put his fork down on his tray and tapped his temple with his finger. "I think, and then I try to find a solution with the information I have at hand."

"Then how about sharing your information with us?" Ed suggested.

Einstein continued to smile. "You wouldn't understand it."

"We wouldn't understand it?" Ed's temper flared. Wendy laid an arm across his shoulder.

David shook his head. The Helios expedition had been chaotic, but it looked like smooth sailing from where he stood now. Ed had been completely right about one thing: this mission was nothing but a kamikaze assignment. They hadn't had the slightest idea what they might be confronted with, and now they were all going to die. In a couple of weeks they'd have eaten the last of the food and would begin starving to death. David had run the numbers through the computer. By the time they took the last five packaged meals out of the cabinet, the number of Hubbles they'd flown would have twenty-five zeros.

In the meantime, they saw nothing but darkness outside the bridge windows. For one thing, they were flying so fast, you could no longer make out structures with the naked eye; furthermore, the event horizon caused by the curvature of their space-time bubble had gotten larger. Light only reached the sensors through a small slit. But after editing the images from the high-power telescope on his computer, David could still see the characteristic structure of outer space. Galaxy clusters and voids, distributed somewhat unevenly. Even here, further from home than the human brain was able to grasp, the universe looked the same as it did from Earth. Were there people out here in the Hubble volumes they were racing through this very second? Or at least sentient beings similar to humans? A crazy thought crossed David's mind, and he laughed out loud.

"What's so funny?" Ed asked in the same tone of voice he'd just used to chastise Einstein.

"I was just thinking about the consequences of an infinite universe."

"Such as?"

David grinned at him. He couldn't help it. "For one, we would have infinite duplicates."

Ed looked at Wendy as if David had finally lost his mind.

"Don't you get how huge infinity is?"

"Apparently not," Ed muttered, but he looked at David with curiosity in his eyes.

David inhaled and exhaled slowly. "Our Hubble volume has a fixed spatial content. Quantum mechanics teaches us that we can't break it down into random subsets.

Which means our local universe has a limited number of states that define it."

"But if we fly through numerous Hubbles at the speed we're going ..." Grace continued. She seemed to have understood the implications.

"... then at some point we'll reach a Hubble volume that just by chance is identical to ours," David finished, grinning at Grace, who grinned back.

"A true parallel universe!" Wendy exclaimed.

David nodded.

"How many Hubbles would we have to cross to come across one?"

David shrugged his shoulders. "I don't know. A lot."

Ed's smile was strained. "If we continue to accelerate at this rate, we'll be covering plenty of ground in under one second."

David nodded slowly. "Yeah, but by then we'll be ..." He stopped.

There was an uncomfortable silence.

"... dead," Ed finally completed his sentence.

Chapter 27

"I wonder if we shouldn't just break one of them," Ed said quietly, his gaze resting on the antimatter container in its holder.

Grace, who was with him in the propulsion module, looked from him to the container and back again. "Suicide?" she screeched. "Has it really come to that already?"

Ed sighed. "Just an idea. But if it goes on like this ..."

Another week had passed, and by now they'd passed through trillions of Hubble volumes. At some point they were going to have to admit that there was no longer any way out. Even if Einstein somehow found a way to repair the propulsion module, they didn't have enough time to brake, turn around, and fly back home. Even rationed, their provisions wouldn't last. Why not end it all now? Since they were doomed no matter what, you couldn't even consider it suicide from a moral point of view. The only question was how long they should wait.

"Do you want to see the latest recordings from the surveillance camera?" Grace asked.

Ed shrugged his shoulders. "Anything to see?"

Grace shook her head. "Nothing we haven't seen a hundred times before. Einstein pondering over some notes. Einstein smoking a cigar. Einstein sleeping."

"Then I'll pass," Ed answered. He had been hoping for better results from the surveillance, but it looked like Einstein only retreated to the sensor module to get some peace and quiet. He hadn't once touched the hidden console and Ed asked himself why the aliens had installed it at all.

"How you doing?" Grace asked quietly.

Ed smiled. There'd been a time when the engineer hadn't given a flying fuck how he was doing. Sharing a spaceflight definitely brought people together. And this was far from a normal spaceflight, that was for sure. "Terrible. How are you?"

She smiled back at him, and shrugged. "Terrible."

"Well, one more thing we've got in common."

Together, they laughed quietly.

Suddenly Ed heard a sound behind him and turned around. It was David, floating in through the hatch. The kid was white as a sheet.

"What is it this time?"

"The stars," David stammered. "The stars have disappeared."

The sentence sounded all too familiar to Ed, and he would have thought David was joking, but his expression made it clear that he was not. "What are you talking about?"

"Come and see," David croaked, turning around and pushing off from the hatch.

Ed glanced quickly sideways at Grace and followed David. As they entered the connecting module, the door to the sensor module opened and Einstein peeked out sleepily. "Is something wrong?"

Ed ignored him.

"Follow us," Grace ordered.

When Ed entered the laboratory, David was already at his console. Ed stopped himself with a handheld and positioned himself to the left of the young physicist. Grace and Einstein stopped at his right. Wendy also entered the module.

"And?" Ed asked.

David pointed to the large monitor. His hand was shaking. "I just looked at the latest telescope data. The space around us is completely empty."

"What do you mean, 'empty'?" Grace wanted to know.

"There's nothing there. No galaxies, no stars, no matter. We're moving through absolutely empty space. This part of the universe is completely different to anything we've ever seen before."

"Maybe there's just something wrong with the telescopes," Grace suggested.

"No," answered David. "The sensors are intact."

"How can you be so sure?" Ed asked.

David flipped a switch and the monitor showed a pattern of red and blue spots.

"That's the cosmic microwave background again, right?" Wendy asked.

"Yes, but look at the numbers. Do you see those values?"

Grace made a surprised sound.

"Very interesting," Einstein said.

"0.006 Kelvin?" Grace asked.

"Yes," David answered. "In our solar system, and everywhere else I've measured up until now, that value was three Kelvin, or three degrees above absolute zero."

Ed sighed. "And what does that mean?"

"Three degrees above zero is the temperature of the universe. The value is a result of the photons that escaped from the plasma of the Big Bang at the moment the universe became transparent. The value decreases as the universe expands, because the concentration of photons becomes lower. There's only one possible conclusion."

"Which is?" Ed asked.

"Flying in the face of everything we thought we knew, the universe is not homogenous. Some zones are completely different."

"And we've entered one of those zones?" Wendy asked.

"Looks like it." David flipped through varying modes on his monitors. He entered something into his console, and the clock on the large monitor began to run backward. "There," David said after a while. On the left-hand monitor they could see galaxies and galaxy clusters, as they had for most of the expedition, but the light stopped at about the middle of the monitor.

"Wow. It looks like it was cut off with a ruler," Grace cried out.

"The cosmic microwave background, too," David said, shaking his head. "We've actually hit a domain wall."

"A what?" Wendy asked.

"Up to now, it was just a wild hypothesis by a few crazy astrophysicists, but I'm afraid it's the only explanation. And it looks like we got lucky."

"What's a domain wall?" Ed asked. He'd never heard the term.

David nodded for no reason. "Let me ask you a question first. How does molten metal change into a solid?"

Now Ed was in his element—the properties of materials. "The solidification process begins with crystal nuclei and spreads from there. At the borders of the crystals, the solidified areas meet and … oh!" Ed had understood. Every nucleus here had a different structure and form. "You're saying the universe is made of different crystal nuclei?"

"Looks like it. And the properties of the domain we're flying through now are a bit different than in our corner of the universe. Maybe the fine structure constant values are lower, and no material was able to form after the Big Bang. Whatever it is, this part of the cosmos seems to be a lot older than ours. That's what the low cosmic microwave background temperatures suggest."

"You said something about us getting lucky," Wendy said. "What did you mean?"

David shrugged his shoulders. "The characteristics of this domain could have been drastically different from the ones in our part of the universe. Think about what would happen if the gravitational constants were a lot higher. Each of us might suddenly generate a gravitational field. Because of its mass alone, our ship could have fallen into a black hole."

"A terrifying thought, isn't it?" Einstein said.

"Just because it hasn't happened yet doesn't mean it won't," Ed retorted. "If we've passed one domain border, there are sure to be others."

Einstein shook his head. "The symmetry break of adjacent domains that resulted from the inflation are likely similar. I don't believe their values could be very far apart. No need for us to scare ourselves."

Ed laughed out loud. "No need for us to scare ourselves!" he parroted. "The reason we don't need to be scared is that we're going to die soon anyway. Of starvation, in just a few weeks."

He pushed off from the floor until he was standing

directly in front of Einstein. He hit him on the shoulder hard enough that the physicist grimaced in pain. "Too bad we didn't implode as a black hole, isn't it? Looks like we're missing all the fun!"

Chapter 28

"Darkness," Ed said. "Nothing but darkness for weeks."

He felt Wendy put her hand in his. His first impulse was to pull it away. He'd never been the type to be comforted by physical contact. He always found it slightly unnerving. Even when it had been his wife. But he let Wendy touch him and tried to ignore the warmth of her hand on his skin. With his left hand, he flipped through the modes on his main monitor. He stopped at the navigation display. Suddenly he laughed out loud.

He felt Wendy jump. "What?"

"We're so far from home it can't even be represented in exponents anymore."

"… home," Wendy whispered.

"What'd you say?" Ed asked, turning to look at his crewmate, who sat without moving in Grace's seat, staring through the main windows into the darkness.

"Home," Wendy repeated. "We thought we were far from home when we woke up on the aliens' asteroid. But that was nothing compared to this."

Ed nodded thoughtfully. The distance to their home

planet moved a little bit closer to infinity each day. On the other hand, return had been impossible the second they'd landed on that fucking asteroid. Millions of years stood between them and Earth. Impossible couldn't get any more impossible. They were on a spaceship able to cross entire universes in seconds. But even if the engine were working and could get them back to Earth, not even this ship could turn back time. It was easier to cross billions of light-years in spatial distance than it was to bridge one single second of time.

"How are we supposed to go on?" Wendy asked after a while.

Ed didn't answer right away. What could he say? He decided on the truth. "We won't."

"Is this really the end?" There was no emotion in Wendy's voice. She had probably asked herself this question many times already, and most likely she'd come up with the only possible answer.

"There's nothing more we can do," Ed replied matter-of-factly.

"So we'll starve?" It was more of a statement than a question, and Ed didn't answer. "You miss her, don't you?"

Ed turned, surprised. Wendy was staring at the small photo that he'd stuck onto the console next to a monitor.

Ed nodded. "Yeah, I miss Helen."

"Maybe you should have stayed with her instead of taking off for the edge of the solar system with the Helios."

Ed wasn't sure he wanted to talk about it. It hurt too much to even think about Helen.

"It was all my fault," he said quietly. "I wanted that mission no matter what. If Helen had managed to talk me into staying with her, I would have resented her for it for the rest of our lives. She knew that, so she didn't try. But still she couldn't stand it, so she left me. I don't blame her.

Probably I'd have done the same in her shoes. Our divorce was inevitable from the moment General Westing offered me the Helios mission."

"You make it sound like you had no choice."

Ed shrugged his shoulders. "Maybe I didn't."

"You think our fate is inevitable?"

Ed wanted to laugh, but the air went up the wrong pipe and he coughed. "Fate!" He put all the contempt he could muster into the word. "I don't believe in fate. It's just a straw the weak grasp at in a desperate attempt to make some sense out of this bullshit."

Wendy didn't answer and Ed wondered if he'd somehow inadvertently offended her. "I believe in coincidences and in God's will. Fate, I hate," he added, hoping to conciliate her.

"Isn't God's will just another word for the same thing?"

Ed shook his head. "I don't think God has the time to worry about what each individual idiot is doing. That's our job as humans. Case closed. Mind if I change the subject back to our partners? You still think about Gerry a lot?"

Wendy nodded. "I'm always wondering how his life was after we disappeared. Did he suffer horribly? Did he marry another woman after a while? What did he do ... and how did he die?"

Wendy paused for a long time, but Ed knew she wasn't done yet. "Do you think they held a funeral for us with empty coffins? Whenever I realize that it all happened millions of years ago, I feel like I might go crazy."

"I try to repress it completely. Usually I even manage."

"Still, I wish I knew what happened to Earth—what happened to humanity. The aliens wanted to bring us back when we returned; fill us in on what we missed. I guess that's not going to happen."

Ed nodded. "Nope. Maybe we should have a word with Einstein. He should finally tell us what he knows."

"I'm not sure the aliens ever told him. I bet someone else would have brought us to Earth."

Ed thought he heard something behind him and turned. But both the bridge and the tunnel to the living module were empty. He must have been imagining things. He turned back to Wendy and said darkly: "Those plans have changed now."

Chapter 29

"I've figured out why we keep racing into eternity," David said. "And why all the aliens' probes disappeared."

"Out with it!" Ed said.

David pointed to his monitor. "The event horizon that formed at the edge of our space-time bubble has now enclosed us completely."

"Enclosed us completely ..." Ed repeated.

David nodded. He'd seen it coming. It had just happened earlier than he'd expected. "Yeah, the gravitational pull of the wave is so strong in the direction of flight that not even light can escape when it hits it directly. And the bubble has an equally strong pull in the opposite direction. Most of the light is diverted around the bubble. There's just a small thin area on the side of the ship that lets in light from the outside."

"An area that'll probably also close soon," Grace guessed.

David shook his head. "No, I don't think so. The slit might taper off some, but the phenomenon seems to have come to a standstill."

"I wonder what it looks like from the outside," Grace said.

David scratched his chin. "I've thought about that too, but I can't find a conclusive answer. Probably from the front it looks like a black hole racing through the universe. Whatever falls into it is destroyed and released again from the back as radiation."

"From the back?" Ed repeated.

"Behind us, the potential energy of the bubble is positive, so it probably looks like a white hole."

"A white hole?" Wendy asked.

"The opposite of a black hole," Einstein said. "It repels energy instead of sucking it in."

"They've been completely hypothetical objects up to now, but it makes sense," David said. He was surprised that he could still get excited about physical phenomena, despite the hopelessness of the situation they were in. "Whenever we have a frontal collision with mass or radiation, it's radiated out again from behind. Although not all of it, I presume."

"You presume?" Ed repeated.

David nodded. "Some of the energy that was absorbed remains in the warp bubble. That's why its curvature—and with it our speed—becomes greater. It's a physical process that becomes irreversible once we've reached a certain speed. That's why none of the probes were ever seen again."

Ed snorted. "Not like knowing that does us any good. We're still going to die. We've used up almost all our provisions. We have four more weeks."

"One more thing," David said. "We passed more domain borders. Two yesterday alone."

"Two?" Wendy said in surprise. "How fast are we going now?"

David waved his hand dismissively. "So fast there's no good way of expressing it in numbers. In one second we pass billions of Hubbles. Anyway, the new domains were both without mass, their fundamental constants couldn't support life."

"Maybe our domain was the only one in the universe that could," Wendy suggested.

"Possibly," David said. "It certainly looks like the domains become less hospitable to life the further we get from our own."

"You think those domains are also threatened by vacuum decay?" Ed asked. His expression had gone from confused to thoughtful.

"Probably," David said. "They're all part of the same universe, even if it is divided up. But that's not what I wanted to show you."

"What did you want to show us?" Einstein asked. David stared at him, and had to shake his head. Einstein's eyes were wide-awake and curious. He didn't seem in the least bit worried by, much less scared of, the increasingly abstruse image of the universe they were finding. Sometimes it even seemed to David that he was amused by their reaction to the unknown. What went on inside his head?

David turned back to his console and his monitors. He pulled up an image he'd saved. "I have some new pictures of the cosmic microwave background. Let me know if you notice anything." For his part, he'd first thought he was seeing artifacts of the signal processors.

"There's a bright line," Grace said.

David nodded. A white line ran diagonally across the image, easily visible against the blue and red dots. He advanced to the next image.

"Another line," said Ed. "Weird. What is it?"

David hit a button and a new image appeared.

"There's an orange spot," Wendy remarked.

"I even have a video of this one. Hold on a sec." David pushed a button. It was more like a series of images than a real video. The orange blotch, a circle with a jagged edge, appeared on the right of the screen. It moved to the left in steps until it vanished from the screen.

"What was that?" Ed asked.

"Defects," Einstein whispered.

David nodded.

"Excuse me?" Grace asked.

"It looks like we've reached a truly strange region of our universe," David replied. "What we just saw were defects in space-time. The line is a cosmic string, the orange plane is a two-dimensional topological defect. They appear bright because they send out radiation."

"Radiation?" Ed repeated. "What kind of radiation?"

"Mostly gamma rays at the low end of the spectrum. Not that I know how they're created."

"And what does it tell us?" Ed asked.

"It means our universe is a lot more irregular and stranger than we thought. Most importantly, it's not perfect, otherwise there wouldn't be any defects."

Ed shook his head. "How can the universe have defects?"

"Could you explain it?" David asked Einstein.

Einstein looked at David for a long time as if deciding, and then shook his head, earning a dissatisfied grunt from Ed.

David sighed. Not for the first time, he asked himself whether Einstein wasn't completely up to speed on modern cosmological theory, or whether he just didn't want to talk about it. "It's also connected to inflation. Computer simulations were run to study the possibility of topological defects, with the result that certain conditions during the transitionary phase—the end of inflation—could lead to discontinuities in space-time." David tried to think of an analogy. "Think about making glass. If molten glass hardens too quickly, it forms cracks. This is similar."

"OK, but what do the defects mean? What happens if we collide with one, for example?" Grace asked. She looked somewhat pale.

David couldn't blame her for being afraid. They'd already determined that nothing happened to their ship in its bubble when it collided with normal mass, but topological defects in space-time were another thing entirely. "Good question. One-dimensional defects like cosmic strings have a high density, but we should be able to survive a collision. Probably the string would be destroyed or cut by our warp field. I worry more about the two-dimensional defects."

"What's the difference?" Wendy asked.

"One-dimensional strings stretch across space like thin threads. Two-dimensional defects are planes, as $_s$as we saw." He thought for a moment. "Actually, the domain borders we passed are also two-dimensional defects that divide the universe into different parts, but whatever we saw on the monitor is something else entirely. I can't say what for sure. It emits a lot of gamma radiation, which worries me. It's possible that we're looking at two-dimensional singularities. Then we might not survive a collision."

"If we keep accelerating and there are more and more of those things, it's only a matter of time until we hit one," Ed said.

David nodded. It was a logical deduction. "Yeah, looks like it." He looked at the right-hand monitor, which continuously generated new telescope images. Glowing yellow-orange planes were appearing more and more frequently on the screen. David was surprised how inimical to life the cosmos was out here.

The universe sure was immense. Much larger than people had ever imagined. But the more David thought about it, the surer he was that it was not infinite. But it didn't curve in on itself, as Einstein and the aliens had assumed. The further they went, the more defects there were. What would happen if at one point they ran into a defect that surrounded the entire universe? David shook his head. Nobody had ever proposed that. It was a little like thinking there was a wooden fence at the end of the universe. But if it was true, the universe would be finite after all. Kind of like a bubble whose outer skin was made of an infinitely dense singularity. It they hit that, they would die for sure. If they didn't collide with one of those defects first.

Chapter 30

There, another one!

David hit the pause button on his console and froze the image. The orange ellipse was now in the middle of the monitor, with the usual blue-and-red pattern of the CMB behind it. The edges of the defect were blurry, but David was pretty sure that was only because of their own monstrous velocity. He was surprised you could make out anything at all in a telescope image. He clicked on the middle of the elliptical shape and pressed the analysis button. Characteristic spectrum curves appeared on another monitor. But the automatic classification into possible elements failed, and David knew why. The spectrum on the monitor hadn't been created by any phenomenon known to humankind. Where did the radiation come from? There was no mass in this part of the universe that could react with the defect. Did it have something to do with the ominous vacuum energy? Was the light maybe even from another universe? Some complex theories assumed that defects were caused by the collision of two universes. Humanity had not yet thought up any useful theories for the things that happened out here at the rim of the cosmos.

"Lost in thought again?"

David spun around. Grace had entered from the connecting module and stopped herself on his console. She smiled as she lowered herself into the seat right next to his. David got goose bumps as he felt her warmth. He nodded in the direction of the monitor. "It's beautiful and fascinating. But at the same time terrifying, because you know that sooner or later we're going to collide with one of those things."

"You really think that'll be the end of us?"

David nodded. "If they really are two-dimensional singularities, then they'll destroy our warp bubble." He snapped his fingers. "Like that."

"How much warning will we have?" Grace asked. Her smile had frozen on her face.

"None," David answered tersely. "We're going too fast. What we see on the monitor are only computer renderings of what's already behind us. It'll be over just like that."

"At any moment?"

David took a deep breath and exhaled slowly. There still weren't that many defects. And most of them they passed from a great distance. But there were more of the uncanny planes, and they were getting larger. There was no way of knowing when it would happen. He hadn't tried to run a statistical analysis.

He nodded.

"It's a strange feeling," Grace said after a while, not moving her eyes from the monitor. "I mean thinking about the fact that we could die at any moment. Just stop existing. Just like that. Her voice was matter-of-fact and disengaged. Like she was talking about someone else's life, not her own.

David didn't answer. What could he say?

"My father died of cancer when I was a kid," Grace said, still staring at the monitor. "I was twelve. My mother passed away years earlier. My father didn't know where to send me during the exams and treatments, so I went with him to the clinic. Every time. I sat next to him when they jabbed the chemo drip into his arm. I read comics. He stared at the wall. I was so bored." She turned her head and looked at David.

"Then came a day I'll never forget as long as I live. We were in his oncologist's office again. Dad was sitting across from the doctor at the desk, I was sitting on a chair at the back of the room. Up until then, the doctor had always tried to boost my father's spirits, get him psyched for the next treatment. That day, he told my father he should get his affairs in order. Dad was silent for a while, then he nodded and asked how long he had. The doctor shrugged and said he didn't know. It could be over any day. That was the moment I realized it wasn't a game; it was serious. That my time with my father was limited—you could count it in days. I was devastated. Later, I was ashamed of reacting the way I did, since it was my father who was facing the end, not me. For years I wondered how he had felt at that moment." She swallowed. "Now I know."

"I'm sorry," David said. He didn't know what else to say.

Grace laughed softly and took his hand. "You're sorry? Why should you be sorry? You're in the same boat as I am."

David shrugged and enjoyed the warmth of her hand.

"There's something the two of us still need to deal with," Grace said finally.

David nodded. They hadn't spoken about the embarrassing situation since it had happened a few weeks ago. David was just as happy to sweep the whole thing under the rug. But enough time had passed that it wasn't quite so bad to think or talk about it. "I was kind of ... I thought ... anyway, I'm sorry."

Grace smiled tentatively. "Nothing to be sorry for. I like being desired as much as the next girl. But I was a bit surprised. I mean, you knew I had a girlfriend back on Earth."

"Well, you could have been ... bisexual."

Grace stared at him again with that equivocal look he so feared. "I am bisexual."

David knew the expression on his face must be pretty stupid, but what was he supposed to do now? Make a fool of himself again?

Grace brushed her thumb across his hand and adrenaline flooded his body. Before he knew what he was doing, he bent forward and felt her lips on his.

"Come with me to the propulsion module."

"Why?" he asked, and immediately could have slapped himself.

"I have a sleeping bag there. Who knows whether we'll have another chance to spend some time together, just the two of us." She let go of his hand and pushed herself off of the stool. In a daze, David followed her to the propulsion module.

Chapter 31

Ed awoke from a nightmare with a start the moment the red alert siren sounded. Years of training had honed his reflexes, and before he was completely awake his eyes were already scanning his console. The Magellan systems all seemed to be in order. The life support system was also working. There was a red light glowing on Grace's console, and he leaned over to see what it was. Something was wrong with the thermal control. He pressed a button next to his monitor and the display changed. The external sensors had registered a rise in temperature, but only on one side. Strange. And where were the others? They should have all headed to the bridge immediately as soon as the main alarm sounded.

"What's wrong?" Wendy asked behind him. He heard her seatbelt click as she strapped herself in.

"External temperature is rising," Ed said.

"The external temperature? How could that be? Sensor error?"

"I don't think so, there's too many of them for that. Where the hell is Grace?"

"We're here."

Ed turned around. Grace was floating into the cockpit, David close behind her. Both were sweating. David was having difficulties closing the zipper of his mission outfit. Had he been sleeping? Whatever.

"Grace, check the external sensors. One side of our ship is registering a rise in temperature. Check the thermocouples and the ADC."

Grace lowered herself into her seat. The console had activated itself when the alarm went off. She pulled up multiple displays. "Systems are all working. Temperatures portside are rising. But they're within range. Change of fifty Kelvin. The curve is flattening, shouldn't get much warmer."

"But where's the heat coming from? David! What do the sensors say?"

The young physicist didn't answer.

"Hello," Einstein said as he floated onto the bridge. "Is everything OK?"

"Shut up and sit down!" Ed ordered. "David?"

"Hold on a sec," David croaked. "I need a minute."

Goddammit, what was going on? Something was bothering Ed, but he couldn't put his finger on it.

"Did anybody look out the window?" Wendy asked. She sounded surprised.

Ed looked up. That's what was different! He'd gotten used to not looking out the bridge windows, since there'd been nothing to see. And there ought to be nothing to see now—so what was that red glow all of a sudden? It was still dark out, but the black was somehow reflecting red light. The window frames were veritably radiant.

"There's a source of strong infrared light out there," David said finally. "It goes all the way into the visible spectrum."

"I can see that for myself. But where's it coming from?" Ed asked. He wasn't sure how to react. Something strange was going on.

"It's coming from the thin slit in the warp bubble that isn't covered by the event horizon."

"Where is it?" Ed asked.

"To our left."

Ed reached for the control stick and began rotating the ship. Long seconds later, a bright red sliver of light could be seen in the main window.

"What the hell is that?" Ed mumbled.

"It looks almost like we've flown into a red giant star and now we're stuck inside," Grace croaked.

"David!" Ed jumped. Did he really just yell? He was simply overwhelmed by their predicament. Neither his astronaut training nor his experience on multiple missions had prepared him for this.

"How the hell should I know what it is?" David screamed back.

Shit, what had they gotten themselves into now? Ed had figured they'd collide with something at some point. With a string or one of those two-dimensional topological defects. And he'd counted on the result being their split-second death. "Did we cross another domain border? $_{Ha}$What did we do, land in some region of the cosmos filled with red shit?"

"Quite possibly," David answered. "The telescopes aren't showing anything. The red light is completely homogenous, as if its source were right outside our bubble."

"What does Occam's Razor say?" Einstein prodded gently, sounding as if it cost him a lot to say anything at all.

"The simplest explanation is usually correct," David

answered automatically. He'd heard that question often enough in his life as a physicist.

"Which would be?" Wendy asked.

"That the red light is coming from right outside the warp bubble."

Ed turned around. "What's that supposed to mean?"

David's brow was furrowed. Einstein smiled at him. "Perhaps the event horizon has engulfed our ship completely. I mean, days or even weeks ago," he offered.

David shook his head energetically. "Then we shouldn't have received any telescope images since then."

"Think again," said Einstein, sounding for all the world like a professor speaking to a student.

Ed felt his blood pressure rising sharply. "If you have an idea, spit it out!"

Einstein cleared his throat and pulled at his tie. "Light can fall into a black hole, it just can't get out. If a spaceship fell into one, it could still look out. It would still see any light that crossed the event horizon after it."

"Are you saying we're inside a black hole?" Wendy asked.

Einstein shook his head. "That was only an analogy. But I do think an event horizon has separated us from the rest of the cosmos for some time now. We are inside our own bubble of space-time. A miniature cosmos if you will, that we've created with our warp drive. The only connection to our old universe was through a thin slit, not unlike a wormhole."

"Well, you wanted to create your own universe. Looks like you managed it," said Ed, not bothering to keep the sarcasm out of his voice. "Just a little small, your cosmos."

Einstein didn't deign to answer, looking instead expectantly at David, who was thinking feverishly. "That still doesn't explain the red light from outside." He typed some commands on his keyboard and shook his head at his monitor. Ed couldn't see what he was looking at. "The spectrum of the red light is similar to that of the two-dimensional defects. There are only slight deviations, a little like the cosmic microwave background."

Einstein nodded. "And what do you deduce from that?"

David stared unblinking at the monitor. He shook his head again. "The CMB pattern stems from quantum fluc-tuations during the phase transition that ended inflation. If both phenomena have the same cause, that can only mean that ... that ..." The color drained from his face. "No. That's not possible ..."

"What?" Ed asked. "Spit it out already!"

David looked in his direction, but he wasn't looking at him. "Is that possible? Could it be?"

"I have come to the same conclusion," Einstein said.

"Then we've reached the end of the road," David whispered.

"What makes you say that?" Ed asked, unsure he wanted to hear the answer.

David stared right through him. "We've flown through a defect."

Ed didn't understand. "Flown *through* a defect? I thought they were so dense we would die if we collided with one."

David shook his head in slow motion. "I thought so too, but I was wrong. They're not only topological defects. They're the borders of our universe and you can pass through them, just like we passed through the domain borders. At least, you can pass through them if you happen to be traveling faster than the speed of light."

"You mean they're like gates you can fly through?"

"Gates. Good analogy," David said. He spoke so quietly, Ed barely heard him.

"So where are we? Another universe?"

David shook his head. "We're at the source of all universes. We've crossed through a space-time defect into inflationary space."

"That's impossible," Grace said. It was more like a scream.

David must have lost his mind, there was no other explanation. "Inflation took place right after the Big Bang. You said so yourself. Nanoseconds later our universe was formed and the inflationary phase was over," Ed said.

David was still looking right through him. "True. For our universe. But in other parts of the multiverse, inflation continued. It's never-ending. Like a waterfall dropping into eternity. Little bubbles constantly form on the surface that all fall back in on themselves immediately. Get it? Each of those bubbles is a universe. Ours was one of them; and now we've left it. We've flown out of our universe through a topological defect."

Ed said nothing while he tried to digest David's words. Grace and Wendy were also silent. Only Einstein tittered to himself.

"We've left the bubble of our universe and now we're riding a thunderous waterfall toward eternity," David whispered. "This is the end of our journey. There's no going forward. We'll be stuck here forever."

"Maybe we could get back if we fixed the engine," Wendy said tentatively. "Back to our universe, I mean."

David shook his head again. "There's no return. Inflation expands the space between universes with an unimaginable force. Even time means something else here. Our universe doesn't even exist anymore. It's moving away from us at infinite velocities—spatially and temporally."

"Well, maybe we'll fall into another universe by chance," Wendy whispered, and started to sob.

"You obviously haven't understood what I just said," David said, his voice cracking. Ed was reminded of the diving pool in Houston, long ago, in another universe, when David had had a panic attack brought on by claustrophobia. He was headed that way again if he didn't calm down.

"Take a deep breath," Ed said, trying to sound composed. He even managed to smile. In reality, he was about to lose it himself. If we're really in inflationary space, why couldn't we land in another universe, ours or an unknown universe?"

David raised and slowly dropped his shoulders. "This is where universes are born and die. Even if a new universe was born right next to us, it would immediately be cut off from inflationary space-time and fly off at an incredibly fast speed."

"And how fast are we going now?" Grace asked.

David laughed hysterically. "We're not! Warp drive might be working, but it has no effect here, except that the event horizon of our bubble protects us from the direct impact of inflationary space. The propeller doesn't do anything either when a ship falls over the edge of a waterfall."

Ed thought it didn't really all fit together. "If the forces inside inflationary space are so great, why don't they just burst our space-time bubble and send us all to hell?"

"Because strictly speaking, we're not in inflationary space. We're in our own miniature universe, created by our warp drive. Its event horizon forms a border to the outside. The density of the vacuum energy in our pocket universe is lower, that's why the inflaton field collapses at the event horizon. The only things that reach us are the particles associated with the inflationary field. They're unstable and decay immediately into photons, which we see as a red glow."

Ed shrugged his shoulders. The theory wasn't really important anymore. The only thing that mattered to them was that they'd reached their final destination.

Though it seemed like Wendy hadn't realized that yet. "And what ... what do we do now?"

David didn't answer right away. "Nothing. We're stuck here. There's no going forward or back. Our spacecraft in its mini-cosmos is surrounded by infinitely quickly expanding space and is being pushed further and further into the infinite future."

"Like a sailboat in the Middle Ages that fell over the edge of the Earth ..." Grace rasped.

"Not a bad comparison," David said.

"Einstein." Ed stared at the Nobel Prize winner. "What have you got to say?"

He stared back at him for a long time and then shook his head. "I don't have anything to add."

Ed hadn't expected any other answer. He turned to Grace who was staring absently at the red light outside the window. He nodded. "Then we'll starve here. At least we know where we're at."

Chapter 32

"That's it," Ed said, passing David a tray of chili. "From now on, we eat only dirt."

He meant of course the meals that no one liked. The tuna that tasted like chicken or the chicken that tasted like tuna. Or the broccoli with mashed potatoes, which had given Ed cramps the last time.

He didn't add that there would be nothing left at all after a week of inedible meals. Ed stared morosely at Einstein, who was slurping chili loudly from his spoon and already had drops of red sauce on his mustache. He wished he could just not feed the physicist. He wasn't a member of their team. Ed shook his head. He didn't want to get worked up about Einstein today.

Wendy took a spoon from an indentation on the tray. The chili stuck to it despite weightlessness, because of the liquid's adhesive force. She let the spoon float in front of her face and looked at it thoughtfully. "Shouldn't we have kept the chili for our last meal?"

"That would be even worse," Grace said bitterly.

In the two weeks since they'd landed in inflationary

space, she'd lost even the last furtive trace of hope. Denial had given way to desperation, desperation had turned to rage and rage had finally become bitter acceptance of the terrible truth.

Ed had sat for a long time in the cockpit, thinking about their imminent end. He'd reckoned with it since takeoff, but he had been sure their end would come quickly. He had hoped to not even notice it. Now that hope had been dashed and all that remained were weeks, or maybe of even months, of slow starvation. It was worse than his worst nightmare. That's not how he wanted to die. Before that happened, he would enter the airlock without a spacesuit and open the outside hatch. They'd avoided the topic until now, but it was time to talk about it. He was just wondering how best to approach the issue, when Wendy beat him to it.

"Shall we put an end to it?" she asked.

"I don't want to starve," David said quietly. "It sounds harmless, but I think it's one of the most horrible and slowest deaths there is. The body eats itself up."

Ed nodded. "I'm not dying of hunger, I can promise you that."

"Me either," Grace said, her voice full of grim resolve.

"Too bad," Einstein said.

Ed looked at him with raised eyebrows. "Excuse me?"

"I said too bad we're in this situation now—now that the engine is working again."

Ed thought he had heard wrong. "What did you say?"

"We can control the warp drive again. I can turn it on and off."

David stared at Einstein with his jaw dropped.

"Now of all times? When we're stuck here?" Wendy asked, somewhat hysterically.

Einstein shrugged his shoulders. "It must be the higher

vacuum energy of the inflationary space. I can manipulate the field more quickly than ever before."

"What good does that do us?" Ed asked, but the question was rhetorical.

"None," Einstein admitted.

"Then why don't you just keep your mouth shut?" Ed snarled.

"It's not his fault," David said. "The aliens only borrowed the technology from another species, they didn't even completely understand it themselves. At least now we really know what happened to the probes. They're not speeding through an infinite universe; probably they all just fell into inflationary space through some defect. Each in its own little universe, cut off from our world. He flipped through his displays. "But one thing's weird."

"What?" Grace asked.

"I'm still getting data from the microscopic wormhole in the sensor module. It somehow seems to have kept its connection to its counterpart on the asteroid. From the data, the aliens should be able to draw the right conclusions about what happened to us. They'll see that the universe isn't a hypersphere where you can return to the beginning by following a geodesic line. They won't send anyone else out on a journey like ours."

"Fat lot of good that does us," Ed said angrily. "Or any of the other assholes they sent out with us. Right, Einstein?"

He received no answer, and sighed. "We've gone off on a tangent. We're facing the end and we need to decide whether to speed it up to avoid dying of starvation. You all voted yes."

"I didn't," Einstein replied. But he said it quietly.

Ed ignored him. He couldn't care less what the physicist thought. "We should decide whether we all want to go together or leave each person to their own devices."

Wendy gulped. "But how? I don't think I can hurt myself."

Ed swallowed. He tried to repress the fact that he was talking about suicide and see it as a purely technical problem. "There's nothing in our first aid kit. The sleeping pills aren't strong enough. And there are no weapons on board. The best method is probably to open the airlock—each of us can do that without a spacesuit."

"Would it be fast?" Grace asked matter-of-factly.

Ed nodded. "Explosive decompression. Presses the air out of your lungs. Within seconds you'd be unconscious and you'd never realize you were suffocating. Pretty humane way to go, actually."

"Could we do it for the whole spaceship at once?" David asked. His voice was devoid of emotion.

Grace nodded. "We could activate the emergency jettison of the propulsion unit without first closing the hatch."

"What about the antimatter itself?" Ed asked. "Couldn't we use it to detonate the spaceship? That'd be faster."

Grace shook her head. "Theoretically the batteries in the magnet trap can be manipulated, but in reality they're integrated into the containers. I don't know any way to get to them with the tools we have on board."

"Couldn't we just break the containers?"

"No. They were constructed to withstand even the explosion of the booster. No way on earth we can break them with our tools."

"So that leaves either the airlock for each of us individually, or jettison the propulsion module."

"Looks like it," Grace confirmed.

"There's one thing I don't like about it," David said.

Ed turned to look at him. "What?"

"Our corpses will remain in this mini-universe, speeding through eternity."

Ed laughed out loud. It was a bitter laugh. "Our own miniature universe for a tomb. Not bad."

Chapter 33

"Hey Ed," David said, floating into the cockpit. David had spoken quietly, unsure whether their commander was sleeping.

But Ed was awake and turned around slowly, giving David a half-hearted smile. A smile that didn't fool David in the slightest. "Hi David, everything OK?"

David couldn't suppress a giggle. Obviously nothing was OK anymore. "Sure, fine. Just wanted to check in with you." Actually, he wasn't really sure why he'd come. Probably because he just couldn't stand being alone in his laboratory anymore.

Which was strange. He'd always liked being alone. He'd never had trouble finding things to do—his research or, since leaving Earth, working with the instruments on board first the Helios and then the Magellan. He'd enjoyed thinking about the meaning of the measurements and data that flitted across his monitors.

But ever since they'd left their universe and it was clear that in a matter of days, they'd be dead, he was plagued by loneliness. All his thoughts were melancholy. He was still young. In his twenties, goddammit. And now it was all over? His death didn't even have a meaning. They hadn't managed to circle the universe and bring the aliens the data they needed for their scheme. For the first time ever, he truly wished he had turned down the Helios mission. What if he had just said no to Wyman and stayed at home with his parents? Maybe he'd have lost the job at Centauri, but there were always interesting opportunities popping up for a young physicist of his caliber. He could have worked at a university. Even Stanford or Berkeley. There were a whole slew of fascinating projects out there that had nothing to do with space travel. The Neutrino Observatory in Antarctica for example. Or the Mauna Kea observatories. Then he could have lived in Hawaii—that would have been something. He would have had a career, maybe someday he even would have met a wonderful woman and started a family.

OK, then he'd already have died billions of years ago, but he would have had a life. Instead, he was just hanging out in a tin can waiting for the end. There was just one way to describe his situation: fucked up.

"Well, don't just float there at the entrance," Ed said, his voice gentler than usual. "C'mon in and sit down."

David pushed himself off the handheld and floated slowly to the front. He sat down at Grace's console without activating it. Instead, like Ed, he stared out the windows. Their commander had again turned the ship so it was facing the thin sliver of space-time that connected them to inflationary space. The red light seeping from the event horizon seemed to be almost alive. Like the unfeeling eye of God, who watched them without mercy, waiting for the Last Judgment. David could feel the warmth of the light despite the triple-paned windows.

"It's terrible and fascinating at the same time, isn't it?"

Ed said. "If you stare at it long enough, you fall into a trance. Like you're looking into another world."

"Which you in fact are," David replied. "It's the original light. The source of our and all other universes."

"I wonder what it looks like on the other side," Ed said.

"Beyond the event horizon are forces we can't imagine in our wildest dreams. It's where space and time themselves are born, and pulled apart with infinite might. Universes are born and die simultaneously."

"Sounds like quite a show," Ed said. "Pass the popcorn. Except, if universes are created and destroyed in the same instant, how can they bring forth life like ours did?"

"Time is different there. Every universe that forms creates its own time."

"But you said the microscopic wormhole is still communicating with the wormhole mouth on the asteroid, right?"

David nodded.

"Even now, although our universe is long gone?"

David shrugged his shoulders. "Maybe the aliens will manage to extrapolate the topology of the universe we flew through from the wormhole data. Maybe they got enough information to proceed as planned."

Ed shrugged his shoulders. "We'll never know." He turned his head and looked David right in the eye. "What's going on between you and Grace, by the way?"

David couldn't suppress a grin. The memory alone his body flood with warmth. At least he wouldn't die a virgin. "None of your business, Ed."

Ed mumbled something unintelligible, shook his head and stared out the window again at the red eye of the cosmic inflation.

Chapter 34

"Hi David."

David turned, surprised. He'd heard the hatch, but he'd expected to see Grace or Wendy floating into his module. Einstein hadn't shown himself much in the past days, he was spending most of his time in the sensor module again.

"What are you doing?" the Nobel Prize winner asked.

David looked at the papers in front of him, all filled with small, neat script. He'd felt the need to write a letter. It wasn't addressed to anyone, but he'd been thinking about his parents when he'd written, which is how it read. He'd needed to unburden himself of all his thoughts and feelings. About their mission, which had now come to an end. About his life, which had taken him from the small town he'd grown up in to the end of universe, and which now had come to a dramatic end of its own.

David knew that no one would ever read the letter, but writing it had helped him come to terms with how he'd lived his life. With hindsight, he would take a different path, but he understood why he had taken the steps that had brought him to this point. He knew now that back then he couldn't have done anything besides decide to participate in the mission.

But none of that was any of Einstein's business. "Just some personal stuff." David pushed a page of his lab protocol on top of the handwritten pages.

"OK, OK," Einstein said. "Do you mind if I keep you company for a while?"

David shrugged. "Not at all. Have a seat." He indicated the empty stool.

Einstein lowered himself and strapped himself in. He pointed to one of the monitors. "Collecting data again? Despite our hopeless situation?"

David smiled wanly. "What else should I do? Besides, I'm interested in the values we receive from the event horizon. Maybe they'll tell us something about inflation."

Einstein flashed a row of yellowed teeth. Immediately there was a smell of tobacco. "I like your attitude. I would have enjoyed working with you." He scratched his nose and laid his head to the side. "Back in Princeton, I mean."

"You really remember that time?"

Einstein nodded slowly. "My memories are vague. As if it were a long time ago." He laughed out loud. "But it is a long time ago, isn't it?"

"But you also know what the aliens know," David stated.

Einstein shrugged his shoulders. "Some of it. I was told what I needed to know for this mission."

"What did they tell you exactly?" David asked.

Einstein laughed again. "They didn't actually tell me. I just know it. It was in my brain when I woke up."

Maybe it didn't matter anyway.

"Do you really plan to kill yourselves?" Einstein asked suddenly.

David actually hadn't wanted to think about it anymore. He'd made the decision and he didn't want to give himself a chance to question it.

"Would you rather starve slowly to death?" he asked in return.

Einstein said nothing.

"Are you keeping something from us?"

Einstein's face remained as expressionless as a mask. "I have not told you everything I know. But I have told you everything that is relevant for this mission."

David inhaled and exhaled slowly. "Can I ask you to please answer one question truthfully?"

"You may."

"Will the aliens be able to do something with the data we've gathered on this mission?"

Straightaway, Einstein shook his head: "No."

"So it was really all for nothing," David said bitterly.

Einstein didn't answer, which David took as agreement.

In a few days, their corpses would float though the depressurized spacecraft. For all time. David could hardly stand the thought. He looked at his console. The right-hand monitor showed an image of the red event horizon, taken by a camera. A thought came to him and he turned back toward Einstein. "You said the engine is able to manipulate the warp drive again."

"Yes, that is correct."

"What if we reduce the curvature of the bubble?"

Einstein looked at the glowing red monitor. "The event horizon would disappear."

"And we would be directly connected to inflationary space," David continued, thinking aloud.

They wouldn't be able to withstand the forces on the

other side. Their warp bubble and its entire contents would be destroyed immediately. Gone. No more corpses flying through eternity.

And he bet it would be faster than explosive decompression.

Chapter 35

"How long would it take?" Ed asked.

"Not long," Einstein answered. "After activating the engine, it would only be a matter of minutes before the event horizon dissipated."

Ed was skeptical. He preferred the idea of ending it all with an explosive decompression. Why should he care what happened to his corpse after he died?

"I'm for it," David said. "It would be a clean end, for us, and for the spaceship."

"I don't want my body to remain out here forever in this mini-universe," Wendy seconded. "I'm also for it." Her voice was strangely unemotional. But her face was swollen and Ed could see that she had cried a lot in the past hours.

"I also think we should try it. If it doesn't work, we still have Ed's plan as a fallback," Grace said.

Ed sighed. "You really want to risk having to try to kill yourself twice? Explosive decompression is a dead ringer."

"Literally," Grace said. "No, I'm for trying it with the engine."

Ed turned to look at Einstein. "What about you?"

Einstein pulled at his tie and then realized he'd been addressed. "Oh, I'm for the engine."

Why had he bothered asking? *What the hell.* "OK. We'll try it."

"When?" Wendy asked.

"Soon," Grace answered. "I don't want to spend any more time thinking about it."

"We have one meal left for each of us. Then we will have used up all our provisions and we'll start starving. I propose we do it today after dinner. That still gives us a couple of hours for ... for whatever," Ed said.

He pushed off the floor and floated toward the bridge without another word. There was nothing more to say. The sooner they finished this, the better.

Chapter 36

David leaned back, exhausted. There wasn't much room in Grace's sleeping bag, and he could still feel her skin on his. He wiped the sweat from his brow with one hand, trying not to breathe too loudly. He'd been slower this time than the first time. They must have made love for an hour. No, he corrected himself. You couldn't call it making love. There was no love between them. It was just sex. It was only about satisfying their desires. And about focusing on something else one last time before they died. And now it was over. He had slept with a woman twice in his life and there would be no third time.

"What are you thinking?" Grace asked, beads of sweat on her face.

David grinned. The question was straight out of a book of clichés.

"That at least I won't die a virgin," he answered.

"At least you liked the first time enough to want to do it again."

David forced himself to smile. "True. But it was different than I'd imagined."

Grace raised her head. "Different how?"

"On the one hand, more intense. Some things were like I'd imagined them, but in reality there are more sensory impressions. Smell ... taste ... it was just more intense."

"And on the other hand?"

David looked at her, irritated. "Huh?"

"You said 'on the one hand' ..."

David nodded. "Oh, yeah. Before, I thought it would be a really big thing. My First Time. Like a rite of passage at church. But after it's over, it doesn't seem like such a big deal anymore."

"Because it's not. I mean, millions of people do it every day. Or did. Some events are more memorable. A rocket launch. Your first time in zero G. But sex is still pretty nice."

"Was I good?" David realized immediately how stupid the question was.

Grace grinned. "You were fine. You just need a little more training."

"What's it like to do it with another woman?"

Grace laughed. "Typical male question. It's not that different, even if you do different things. More important than somebody's gender is who you have sex with and how you feel about them."

David shrugged. While he did have to admit he had feelings for Grace, he couldn't say he'd fallen in love with her. He couldn't say "I love you" to Grace without lying. He'd never know what it was like to do have sex with someone he loved. It was unfair.

He felt his body tense. Today was the day he would die. In one hour.

"I can see exactly what you're thinking," Grace said.

"I'm scared."

An uncomfortable silence spread between them. David

still had one arm around Grace. He could feel her warm skin next to his. The touch was comforting in light of their fate.

"Me too," Grace answered.

Chapter 37

"All we have to do is reverse the thrust?" Ed asked. He turned to Einstein, who was floating serenely above his seat. Obviously he didn't think it was necessary to strap himself in.

"Yes, reverse the thrust. That will reduce the curvature of the bubble and the event horizon will disappear."

"Found the counter-thrust," Grace said. "I really just press the button? That's it?"

"Yes," Einstein nodded.

"And in a few minutes, the event horizon will simply vanish?" Ed asked. And they would die.

"Correct," Einstein confirmed. "Just a few minutes."

Ed inhaled deeply and exhaled in one long sigh. "Does anybody want to say anything?" He looked around at his crewmates.

Wendy was staring blankly at the controls on her console. Her face was mask-like, pale and unmoving. David's lips were quivering. The kid was shaking all over. He returned Ed's look and shook his head.

"Let's just get it over with," Grace whispered.

Ed's gaze wandered to the bridge windows. He'd turned the spaceship in the direction of the red light, which seemed to stare back at them; greedy, uncanny, and threatening. Like a wild animal waiting to break out from its invisible cage and devour them. "Congratulations," Ed whispered. "We're all yours, soon."

"What?" Grace asked.

Ed made a dismissive hand movement. "I said it's been an honor flying with you. Now hit the damned button."

Grace's finger approached the touchpad on her console. Her hand was shaking. Her finger hovered over the button for a moment, then she pressed. There were three buzzes, then nothing.

Ed observed his console nervously, but he kept looking back to the windows. There was nothing to indicate the slightest change. Had something gone wrong? Was the engine broken again? He was just about to direct a cynical comment to Einstein when his eyes fell on the red glow. It had gotten stronger, and its circumference was larger. Like it was moving slowly closer. It was working! Their bubble that rode on a gravitational field was shrinking. Ed looked at the clock. Two minutes had passed since the counter-thrust. It probably wouldn't be much longer now. He had no idea what was going to happen, but at least it should be fast. He would simply cease to exist the moment the horizon vanished and the forces of the inflationary space hit them.

The red light continued to grow. As if they were in a car, driving through the dark toward an illuminated red tunnel. It approached slowly at first, then faster and faster. And all without the slightest sound. So this was what it was like to go to hell. It could only be a matter of seconds now. Ed wanted to close his eyes, but the light was so hypnotizing, he simply couldn't take his eyes off it. He even imagined he felt its warmth on his face.

The entire window front was now engulfed in red light. Wendy said something, but Ed didn't understand her.

His eyes fell on the monitor with the external camera images. The red light now surrounded them—as if it really did want to devour them. Although the cabin temperature was a constant seventy-seven degrees, it seemed to be getting hotter. Instinctively, Ed reached for the cabin ventilation controls to turn up the fan, but he never reached it.

Lightning, brighter than a thousand suns! A crash that sounded like they were inside an exploding dynamite factory.

Ed shut his eyes in pain, but it didn't help. The white light penetrated everything. It went through the windows, through the Magellan's aluminum skin, through Ed's eyelids and through the hand he was holding protectively in front of his face.

He could hear a scream through the deafening crash. Some time passed before he realized it was coming out of his own mouth.

Slowly, the racket and the radiance subsided and he could again make out the contours of his fingers. He put his hand down and blinked. Tears tickled the corners of his eyes and gathered on his cheeks.

Then, all of a sudden, the noise stopped. The white light beyond the window became a pallid gleam and quickly transformed into gray fog. They were speeding through the quickly thinning mist at a staggering speed.

"What the fuck was that?" Ed asked, only now realizing with some surprise that he was still alive. Looked like David and Einstein's plan had gone wrong.

"What happened to the red light?" Wendy wanted to know. "Did we not make it into inflationary space?"

"I don't know!" David croaked.

Ed stared out the window. The fog was gone. Outside was nothing but blackness. They were prisoners of the void.

It had all been for nothing.

If they still wanted to commit suicide, they would have to resort to explosive decompression after all. But where the fuck were they? And what had gone wrong?

In the corner of his eye, Ed saw a flash of light that disappeared again immediately. He thought he was seeing things, but then there was a second one. And a third. And one more. It was lightning.

And not only that. Out of nowhere, bright fireflies appeared and zoomed past their windows. A moment later, the sky was full of them, forming swarms and dancing around one another just like on a warm summer evening on Earth. A few of the swarms separated, forming gigantic clouds, while others came together in disc-shaped struc-tures spinning madly around a common center. Dumb-founded, Ed watched the spectacle, until finally he understood what he was seeing. The fireflies were stars being born and forming galaxies in front of his very eyes. "Oh my God," he whispered. "We're in a universe again!"

"I can see that," Grace said hoarsely. "But I don't understand it. Look how fast the stars are created and how quickly the galaxies are forming. We must be watching billions of years go by."

"Look! There's some brighter lightening back there. See it?" Wendy asked. "What *is* that?"

Ed saw it. Between the new stars, some extremely bright red or orange giant explosions were taking place.

"Supernovas," David whispered. "Time is going by so fast, the first stars have already transformed into super-novas. Soon a second generation of stars will be born, able to generate planetary systems, since now there are heavy elements."

"OK, but what the fuck just happened?" Ed asked. "I was prepared to die any second and instead we've somehow entered another universe."

"A new universe," Grace added. "We watched it being born. But how can time pass so quickly?"

"Our warp drive bubble must have entered this new cosmos at a high relativistic speed. That's why time passes much more quickly outside than it does for us. The effect should decrease while our engine shuts down," David conjectured.

"But we didn't travel through time when we started," Wendy objected.

"I don't think it's an effect of the warp drive. It's because of how we entered the cosmos," David said. "We're lucky it happened that way. Our speed, together with the curvature of the warp bubble, allowed us to withstand the conditions after a Big Bang—that was that bright light."

"We flew through a Big Bang?" Ed asked incredulously.

Nobody on the bridge said anything. Ed stared open-mouthed out the window at the miracle of this new cosmos forming in fast-forward before his eyes. It was true, you could see that things were beginning to slow down. The stars rotated more slowly now around the center of the galaxy, which seemed to be directly in front of them. The form was very similar to the Milky Way and numerous round satellite galaxies spun around it further out. It must be made of hundreds of billions of stars. "But how did we get here?" Ed asked again. "What could have happened?"

"I think *we* happened," David whispered. It was hard to understand him.

Ed turned around. David was pale.

"What do you mean?"

"I think we made this universe."

Ed shook his head. How the hell could they make a universe? "Get out!"

"Really. When we decreased the curvature of the warp bubble, the vacuum inside it made contact with the eternal inflationary space. But instead of devouring us like we thought it would, something else happened." David coughed and continued hoarsely. "The potential energy of inflationary space is incredibly high. It strives to lower its energy, like water freezing when it gets colder. But it needs a crystal nucleus. Don't you see? The inside of our bubble was that nucleus. The new universe formed around our bubble. We ourselves caused the Big Bang when we made the event horizon disappear." David laughed out loud.

"What's so funny?" Ed asked.

"Don't you get it?" David continued to laugh and looked at Einstein, who was listening calmly and, it seemed, with interest. "Without meaning to, we've carried out the aliens' plan. We've created a new universe."

Ed's head was spinning. How could that be? How could they simply create a new universe—one that was billions of years old already. Within a half hour, no less. It was crazy.

"And do you know what the best thing is?" Einstein asked, a conspiratorial grin on his lips. "This new universe is stable."

Chapter 38

"It would be a great solar system for humans. Two planets in the habitable zone, both with breathable atmospheres, enough water, diverse flora and fauna ..." David said, scrolling through the sensor data.

"Eden and Paradise," Ed said drily.

"Excuse me?" Grace asked.

"I said Eden and Paradise," Ed repeated. "Good names for the planets. At least as far as we can tell from orbit."

David looked up from his console to the bridge window. The planet closest to the sun was hanging in front of them, about the size of a basketball. The side they could see had a large blue ocean with many small beige islands. A tropical storm circulated gray-white clouds across the southern hemisphere.

When their spaceship had finally stopped a few hours ago, they'd set course for the galaxy in front of them. They'd soon found this remarkable solar system in the arm of the spiral closest to them. It had an A-type sun that shone with a slightly blue light. At a little over nine thousand Kelvin, it was a lot hotter than Earth's long-gone sun, and thus the habitable zone around it was larger. So it wasn't that surprising that two planets seemed habitable for humans. Just a shame there were no humans who could take advantage of that fact. Since they had no landing capsule, the crew of the Magellan had no way of getting to the surface of one of the two worlds. It was more than possible that there were edible plants down there. It made starving up here all the worse, with salvation staring you in the face.

David wasn't hungry yet. Their last rations hadn't tasted very good, but there had been enough and they hadn't eaten that long ago. But hunger would come in the end and then they'd have to follow Ed's proposal. But first, David wanted answers.

He turned to Einstein, who was leaning back calmly in his seat. He was playing with something in his pocket. David assumed it was a cigar. "You claimed this universe is stable."

Einstein turned to him and nodded. "Yes."

"How do you know that? We haven't run any analyses yet."

Now Ed and Grace turned around as well. Ed blinked mistrustfully at Einstein.

"We manipulated the warp bubble to shrink as needed during the inflationary field's transition phase. The Big Bang of this universe was thus modified accordingly."

David shook his head, repeating Einstein's sentences to himself in an attempt to understand them. "But you couldn't know we would be in that situation. How could you have adjusted the warp drive?"

Einstein just smiled.

It was Ed who drew the correct conclusion. "That's where you're wrong, David," the professional astronaut said bitterly. "It was a frame-up. Einstein and his super-smart accomplices knew from the start where we were headed. They planned the whole mission this way. They just never told us. We're pawns in an intergalactic game of chess."

David couldn't believe it. He'd always trusted Einstein and the aliens, at least to some extent. The alien artificial intelligence may have abducted them and kept them from Earth, but David could understand their motives. When the aliens were convincing them to take part in the mission, their reasoning had been logical and understandable, and he'd decided to believe Einstein. Now he felt used and cheated.

"You knew what was waiting for us out there? The domain borders, the defects?"

Einstein pressed his lips together and nodded.

"The whole story about our mission and circling the universe was a lie from the very beginning?"

"Yes."

"But how did you know that the defects led to infla-tionary space?"

"The probes told us that. It was the only possible inter-pretation of the data."

"The probes?" That didn't fit with what Einstein had told him. "But they were all lost."

Ed laughed out loud. "You still have too much faith in his words," he said. "You've had the wormhole technology for a while already. The probes also were fitted with it."

"Exactly," Einstein confirmed. There was no trace of guilt in his voice. He obviously didn't think there was anything wrong with having lied to his crewmates for so long, leaving them in the dark.

Ed loosened his seatbelt and turned himself around on his seat so he could lay his arms on the back, a position that made no sense in weightlessness. "Can I tell you something, smartass?"

"Please do," Einstein answered.

"You were wrong. It was all for nothing."

Einstein didn't seem particularly impressed. "Is that so?"

"Yes, it is so!" Ed screamed so loudly, it hurt David's ears. "You may have a new cosmos that's even stable and can last forever, but it won't do you a bit of good. Because we can't go back and no one can get here from our old universe, if I've understood the physics of this inflationary shit correctly. And we still have nothing left to eat and will starve soon, if we don't jettison our corpses into the new cosmos first."

Einstein still looked unimpressed after Ed's tirade. David was pretty sure Ed's conclusions were wrong. Einstein wouldn't be so calm otherwise. It looked like the aliens had thought of everything. They wouldn't have begun the whole project if it wasn't going to be of use to them. Why create a new universe if the only thing you could bring to it was a tiny spaceship with four unimportant people? David stared at Einstein, who looked serenely back. "There's none of the real Einstein inside you."

The other man shook his head and laughed. "Of course not. The real Einstein has been dead for a very long time."

He'd spent so long with this Einstein. His appearance, his behavior—David couldn't make out the slightest difference to a real person. "You're really just a compound of nanomachines?" David heard the disappointment in his own voice.

"Correct. I'm comprised of over one hundred billion interconnected nanomachines."

David nodded. "That was always your goal, wasn't it?

To bring a population of nanomachines into this new, stable universe. You'll sever your connections, leave the spaceship, and start building a sphere at the next star. Then you can spread across this universe. It's still relatively young, you won't have to worry about competitors."

Ed just grunted.

Einstein turned away and nodded. "You have understood well. I will begin building the first spheres in this cosmos and create enough computing capacity to transfer the legacy of our old universe."

"But where will you get the information?" Grace added.

David knew right away. "Through the wormhole. Of course it's bidirectional. You've had contact with your counterparts on the asteroid the whole time. That's why you were always in your module, isn't it?"

Einstein nodded.

"That's impossible," Grace said to David. "We had video surveillance. He wasn't in contact with anyone. We'd have noticed."

David waved his hand dismissively. "He's made of nanomachines. He doesn't have to sit at a radio console like a human in order to make contact. Probably he has some kind of wireless technology or some way of making telepathic contact while we think he's asleep."

"Asshole!" Ed screamed.

David had already wondered why their commander was being so calm. Probably it had just taken a while for it to sink in. Any second now, Ed would attack Einstein.

"You used us to build a new cosmos for your fucking nanomachines," Ed screamed. "We were nothing but your passive victims."

"Why victims?" Einstein asked innocently.

David had the feeling they still didn't know the whole truth.

"Because we're going to starve here," Ed said.

Einstein shook his head. "You won't starve," he said calmly. He made a theatrical pause, "You will return to your old universe."

Chapter 39

"One second, it must be here somewhere …" Einstein mumbled, floating headfirst in his sensor module. Only his feet, in two different socks, were sticking out of the hatch.

Ed raised one eyebrow and shook his head. He still hadn't understood how they were supposed to return to their universe. Einstein had refused to answer their questions, saying only that they'd find out soon enough. Then he'd unbuckled his seatbelt and floated to the back. Ed had followed him. He didn't trust Einstein not to do something dumb.

"Can you please tell me what the hell you're doing there?" Ed asked. He was mad, because all his fears had been justified. Einstein and the aliens had been toying with them. His first impulse was to punch the doppelgänger, but he forced himself to wait until he knew what he was up to.

"I'm looking for something. Hold on a second. I thought I saw it … no, it's not there either." Ed could hear a slight rustling from the darkened module. "Got it!"

Einstein pushed himself backward. To Ed's surprise, he held out a black USB flash drive in his right hand.

Ed stared skeptically at the storage device. "What's that?"

"That is the raw data about our flight. Written by the module's sensors. The data density is higher than what your consoles received. It might be of use."

Ed shrugged, took the drive and slid it coolly into his breast pocket, while he stared quizzically at Einstein. "Why keep it on a flash drive? It must have been recorded in the sensor module."

Einstein smiled scornfully. "In a few minutes, the sensor module won't exist anymore."

Ed stroked his chin. "And why not?"

Rather than answer, Einstein closed the hatch and, to Ed's surprise, also the hatch of the connecting module. With a jerk of the lever, he locked the door for good.

"What the hell do you think you're doing?" Ed asked.

"We're going to jettison the module," Einstein said, pushing off the floor and floating through the door to the lab. Ed tried to grab him by the jacket, but he wasn't fast enough. He followed Einstein back to the bridge, where the others were sitting at their consoles. Eden still shimmered blue outside the windows.

Ed stood in front of Einstein's seat. "Could you please finally explain what—"

Einstein interrupted him. "You will see in a few seconds. Please take a seat."

Who was actually commander of this ship? Ed could feel his blood pressure rising. "I'm not doing anything until you tell me exactly what the hell—" He fell silent when he felt Wendy's warm hand on his arm.

"Ed, you might as well drop it," she said calmly. "We don't have any choice in the matter."

Ed closed his eyes and took a deep breath. He knew full well that Wendy was right. Without the aliens and their capabilities, they would be stuck here forever. Einstein had promised to bring them back to their universe, however the fuck he wanted to do that. Ed still didn't trust the aliens. But what else could he do? He sighed and floated to his seat. He strapped himself in and then turned to stare at Einstein, who smiled back at him. "Go ahead, do what you want to do," he said, resigned.

Einstein raised his hands almost apologetically. "Oh, I won't be doing a thing. I don't even have a console."

Ed groaned. "OK, what do you want us to do?"

Einstein turned to David. "You'll see a new tab on the sensor console monitor."

"Got it," the young physicist confirmed. "It only has one button. *Decouple.*"

"Exactly," Einstein said with insincere delight. "Please press it."

David looked up. He glanced questioningly at Ed.

Without thinking long, Ed nodded. It's not like things could get much worse, no matter what Einstein was planning. "I can confirm that the hatches have been closed and locked properly. The node module is safe," Ed said.

"If we at least knew what he was doing ..." Grace mumbled.

David touched the button. They could hear a metallic hammering.

Ed turned a button on his console. One of the monitors went on and he could see the image from the external connecting module camera. The barrel-shaped sensor module slowly floated away from them. Ed grabbed the control stick and activated and fired the backboard vernier thrusters to make sure they could get out of the danger zone quickly should the jettisoned module start to spin.

"Sensor module jettisoned," he said to Einstein, without turning around. He kept his eye on the monitor.

"Please fly to a safe distance of sixty miles from the module."

"Your turn, Grace," Ed delegated the task to their engineer.

"Activating the antimatter engine," she said, flipping switches on her console. "Activating in five, four, three, two, one—"

Ed was thrown against his seat and gasped for breath. Grace had throttled the acceleration, but after months in zero G, the pressure was enormous. Luckily, after only a few seconds, Grace turned off the engines and Ed was weightless again. He turned on the monitor for the rear camera and saw the shimmering silver module fall away. "We will have reached the requested distance in just a few minutes. So now you can let us in on the secret. What the hell was that about?"

Einstein smiled. "Actually, I was hoping you'd figure it out for yourselves. You've had enough clues."

Ed groaned. "I am not in the mood for riddles. Just—"

"What is in the module we just jettisoned?" Einstein asked.

"The sensors," Ed answered. He rubbed his temples. He was tired and his head hurt. Too much had happened in too little time. It was impossible for him to concentrate.

"And what else?"

"I haven't the slightest," Ed answered.

"The wormhole," Grace said. "Is that what you're trying to get at?"

Einstein nodded.

Ed understood. There was something else Einstein had been lying about. Well, maybe not lying exactly, but he'd left out one small, but key detail. "You can enlarge it!"

Einstein nodded again. "Turn the ship around!"

Ed reached for the control stick again and rotated the

Magellan slightly. A few seconds later, the module appeared, a silver star in front of the windows. He stopped.

"How far are we?" Einstein asked.

"Seventy-five miles," Grace answered.

"That's sufficient," Einstein said, and turned to David. "Would you please …?"

"Yes, I see the new tab. It's not labeled."

"Press it."

David stretched out his finger.

The second it met the touchpad, there was a bright flash. Ed shut his eyes, blinded, but the brightness had already subsided. When he reopened them, he was looking at a yellow ball of fire, floating in space like a miniature sun.

Ed had no idea what it was. "You detonated the module?"

"A very special detonation."

Ed was about to make a sarcastic remark, but he was sidetracked by the sight of the small sun, which slowly fell in on itself, becoming brighter and brighter. After only a few seconds, the ball of fire disappeared with a blue flash. It was incredible.

"What the fuck was that?" Ed asked.

"Fly back to where the explosion took place. But slowly, please."

Grace fired the counter-thrusters and they crept toward the site.

"We should be able to see it," Einstein said.

"See what?" Ed asked. Einstein didn't answer. Ed looked from his console to the window. His eyes were tearing.

"Ten more miles," Grace said quietly.

At first, Ed thought he was seeing things, but no. There was a spherical area that distorted the stars behind it like a lens. And not only that. It looked like there were stars within the sphere itself.

"That's the wormhole, isn't it?" David asked. His voice was barely audible. Ed thought he knew how the kid felt.

"That is the wormhole," Einstein confirmed. "It leads back to our universe. It has a circumference of over a mile. You can fly through without danger."

"And you?" David asked.

"I will not be accompanying you," Einstein answered. His voice was strangely determined. "I shall leave you now." He unbuckled himself and pushed himself off his seat. Before Ed could say anything, he had disappeared through the hatch.

"Hold on a minute!" Ed screamed, undoing his belt as well. He followed Einstein into their living quarters, the others close behind. Einstein was already opening the airlock. The inner hatch swung open, and Ed realized immediately what the man was up to. "You really want to go out without a spacesuit?"

Einstein laughed softly. "I don't need a spacesuit. I'm only made of nanomachines."

Ed had managed to forget that. "And right away you're going to start filling this universe up with your spheres?"

Einstein shook his head. "No. I'll encircle a few stars with spheres so that there will be enough computing capacity here for you in the future. I'll start with the closest star in the direction the galaxy is turning. I will wait there for you, ready to serve you when you need me."

Ed shook his head. "Ready to serve us? What the fuck are you talking about? We're on our way back, remember?"

Einstein smiled at him. "This is your universe. By *you*, I mean humanity. We sent you out to create it yourselves. A stable universe in which you can spread out, just as we did in the old one. You will start with this solar system. With two habitable planets, it offers ideal conditions."

Ed laughed out loud. "How exactly are four people supposed to spread out? Do we look like two times Adam and Eve to you?" He laughed again.

Einstein shook his head gently. "You still have not understood. The wormhole does not lead to the asteroid we left from. The wormhole mouth on the other side was created when you tried to leave your solar system."

Ed had to repeat the words in his head. Only then did he understand. "You're not saying ...?"

Einstein nodded. "Yes, I am saying. This wormhole will lead you back to your solar system. At the moment you left it."

Chapter 40

"We can really go home?" Wendy asked. Her tone of voice betrayed that she didn't believe a word.

But Einstein nodded.

Could it be? David thought feverishly. Einstein had claimed that the aliens had only shortly before mastered wormhole technology. But that could have been a lie as well. How else could the alien intelligence from the Dyson sphere have created a wormhole within Earth's solar system? After all, they'd been brought to the asteroid via quantum teleportation. For them, no time had passed, because they had moved at the speed of light. The faster something moves, the less time passes. That was, after all, Einstein's special theory of relativity. And the closer your velocity was to the speed of light, the more time approached zero. Maybe the aliens had created a wormhole with two mouths back in their solar system, and sent one of them at almost the speed of light. Then it would be possible for the wormhole they'd carried with them the whole time to actually reach back into their own past. Back to their solar system in the early twenty-first century. "How much time has passed on Earth since we left?"

"Not much," Einstein answered. "A few weeks."

Just a couple of weeks! David shook his head. What an outrageous concept! They'd traveled to the distant future in another galaxy and from there they'd even landed in a new universe outside time. But it had only been an excursion of a couple of weeks. And now they would return home. He would see his parents again, his friends. He could have a future, a life ... his life!

It was Ed who asked the decisive question. "Why didn't you let us in on your plan from the start, you bastard?" His voice quivered.

Einstein smiled. "I did say you would return to Earth when your mission was completed."

"Yes, but we thought you meant Earth in the distant future."

Einstein nodded. "I do realize that, and I apologize. But it was important to us that you keep your eyes open and come to your own conclusions. We didn't want you to be only passengers. Then we could have just placed a wormhole in your solar system as a Christmas present. Simulations showed us that this was the best choice. You are now our missionaries. You shall return to your world and inform them of what is waiting for them in the future."

"Your missionaries?" Ed asked

Einstein nodded. "We wanted you to experience for yourself what it means to leave our universe and build a new one. This new cosmos is yours; you may claim it with the rest of your species. We will help you in any way we can. We shall also make sure that you grow up, and do not destroy yourselves."

"You could have told us that before. I mean, why not

tell us the truth instead of saying we were going to circle the universe. There was no reason to let us think there was no way home."

"Our simulations showed a significant probability that in that case, you would have refused to take part in the mission."

David was convinced not only that honesty would have been the more moral choice, but also that they would have taken part anyway, given the right arguments. Maybe there was still something Einstein wasn't telling them.

"You mean we should relocate to the new universe and there we'll still be under your control? Why the hell should we decide to do that if we're not free?" Ed asked. He'd taken on an accusing tone that reminded David of the discussions between their commander and Q on board the Helios.

But Einstein made a gesture of peace. "We will give you maximum freedom. And when we believe you are ready, we will also give you control over the spheres in this universe. Whereby I believe some time will pass before you are that far along."

David swallowed. The aliens had made them midwives of their own universe. It was the greatest present they could give to humanity. "You planned it all this way, didn't you?"

Einstein nodded again. "Yes. It was part of our task from the beginning. Every intelligent species that manages to reach the borders of their own solar system is sent to the asteroids at the end of time and from there beyond the borders of our universe."

"You mean each species gets their own universe?"

"Exactly. That is the best way to secure our legacy— distributing it among as many universes as possible. It is of course possible that some universes don't make it."

David felt goose bumps rising on his arms. It sounded pretty Darwinist to him. The strong survive and multiply—the weak perish.

Einstein nodded at them and entered the airlock. He turned around one last time. "Treat our new universe well. You will now return to Earth as ambassadors. Tell your story and urge humanity to become wise. There is more at stake than the existence of your little planet. I will be waiting for your offspring one solar system over."

The airlock bulkhead closed. David could see Einstein smiling through the small window. Then, all of a sudden, he was gone. In his place a fine green fog filled the airlock.

An alarm sounded and a red light lit up over the hatch. Then the outside hatch slid open and the mist that seconds before had been Einstein flowed out into the darkness of the new cosmos.

Ed shook his head. "Incredible!"

"I want to go home," Wendy said.

Without another word, they returned to the cockpit and took their places.

"OK. Let's be professional about this," Ed said. "Status?"

Grace nodded. "Spaceship systems are go. Antimatter engine ready at your command."

"Localization?"

David scanned his monitors. "Nothing. All clear."

"What about the wormhole?" Ed said.

David shook his head. "Not being picked up by radar, infrared, or anything else. The only evidence of the anomaly is the optical distortion."

"Good, Ed said. "Let's get going. Since Einstein didn't say anything, I assume we fly straight through it. David?"

David had no experience with wormholes. "No objections."

Ed reached for the control stick. "I'll bring us into position. Grace, at my command fire for five seconds at one G."

Grace's fingers flew across her console. "Ready."

Making small movements, Ed pointed the ship directly at the center of the distortion. "Now," he said calmly.

Grace fired the engines and David was pressed back into his seat. He gasped for breath.

The ball of starlight grew quickly. More and more stars that had been unmoving in front of the window suddenly wandered across the sky as if a lens had been placed in front of them.

"Aren't we going too fast?" Wendy asked.

"No, this is good," Ed said. "We're headed directly for the center."

They must have reached the mouth of the wormhole. David felt like he was inside a crystal ball being slowly turned by a giant. The stars fled backward across the sky. Others came from below, to take the position of the old ones. The entire process was completely still. The only sound was the quiet hum of the life-support system ventilators. It was uncanny.

Suddenly a huge blue area appeared below them that formed into a ball that slowly came to a stop right in front of them.

"Earth"! Wendy exclaimed.

She was right! David blinked. It was mostly blue, with many white splotches. There was land on the right-hand side. David was having trouble orienting himself. Then he recognized the contours. The long peninsula was Baja California of course. And above it California and Nevada, then Oregon. To the left he could make out the Hawaiian Islands.

"He was telling the truth," Ed murmured. "We're home."

"They installed a wormhole directly above Earth," Grace said.

Ed nodded. "Looks like we're in geostationary Earth orbit. It'd be easy to take a shuttle through the wormhole to the orbit of Eden."

"There's just one little problem," Grace said.

David knew exactly what she was referring to. "We still don't have a descent module to get us down to the surface."

Ed nodded. "Yes that's a problem."

"If we can contact Houston, they'll send us a capsule," Grace proposed.

Ed laughed. "Be quite a coincidence if they just happened to have one ready on the launchpad. Unless we're really lucky, we're still going to starve to death. Looking straight at Earth."

"Einstein must have thought of that. The aliens thought of everything else," Wendy said.

"I can allay your fears," a clear voice said suddenly. The voice seemed to come from everywhere at once and David recognized it immediately.

"Q!" Ed blurted.

"Exactly. Glad you made it back."

"Where are we?" David asked. "I mean, when are we?"

"About six weeks after your departure."

David understood immediately. They'd returned to a point in time shortly after they'd launched. At the moment, the information about their bodies was being transmitted to a faraway galaxy as quantum signals. InfInformation that would continue traveling for millions of years. He pushed the thought aside. Dwell on something like that too much, you could go crazy.

"Whatever. Can you please explain how we're going to get to Earth without a capsule?"

"The same way you got to the asteroid on the faraway galaxy."

"You want to beam us down to Earth?" Wendy asked.

"If you don't mind."

"I do mind, but be my guest," Ed mumbled.

"You have chosen a very interesting moment for your return," Q said.

"How come?" David asked.

"Look out the window!"

David raised his head to stare at the blue-brown ball in front of him. At first he didn't see anything unusual and was about to ask, when he saw the lights over the USA. They were moving across the globe like fireflies.

"Holy shit!" Ed cursed. "Atomic missiles! Ours! They're headed to the northwest."

"Then Chinese missiles must be on their way to us," Grace added bitterly.

"Or they will be soon after ours land," David said.

"Q!" Wendy screamed. "Do something!"

For a moment there was silence in the cockpit and David watched in boundless horror as the fireflies crossed Alaska and disappeared over the horizon.

"You may rest assured," Q's voice finally said, "that none of the missiles will reach their targets."

David exhaled. He knew the aliens had the power to intervene in this conflict if they wanted to, but he hadn't been at all sure that they would. On the other hand, they'd just given humanity their own cosmos. What sense would it make to just sit back and watch them destroy Earth?

"I owe you an apology," Ed said quietly.

"What are you talking about?" David asked.

"The aliens. I owe them an apology. I didn't want them meddling in our business, but after what I just saw, it looks like we need a guardian."

"I will not allow humanity to annihilate itself," Q promised. "But it's time you grew up. You have a wormhole in orbit and a whole cosmos to colonize. That should suffice as a meaningful task. You will return to Earth and convince humanity of that. You have time, but not infinite time. The wormhole will provide a stable connection for around one thousand years. After that, it will collapse. By then at the latest, all humans must have left Earth and this universe."

One thousand years! It sounded to him like a very long time. But Q was talking about an entire planet full of people. One thousand years! And then Earth would be as it once had been. Untouched by humans. Perhaps it would again become the paradise it had been when humans first left their cradle. Until the day the universe collapsed.

"I will bring you back to Earth now. Please tell me where I should bring you."

David was still wondering whether he wanted to go to his parents, but Ed knew the answer immediately.

"Bring me to my wife. Bring me to Helen!"

Epilogue

Helen had finished doing the dishes and was just putting the last plate back onto the shelf when she heard a car in the driveway. Looking out the window, she saw a black SUV driving hesitantly toward the house. She washed her hands in the sink, dried them with the dish towel, and walked slowly over to the front door, which stood open to let in the cool air after the hot day they'd had.

When Ed was declared missing four weeks ago, she'd retreated to her sister's summer place in Montana. She'd split up with her new partner shortly after Ed had left for outer space. She was hoping the loneliness of the prairie would help her cope better with her mood swings. She felt horrible about what she'd done.

Of course she'd been angry when Ed volunteered for the new mission despite the promise he'd made. Be that as it may, Ed was the man she had fallen in love with all those years ago. The happy-go-lucky adventurer had maybe gotten a little more staid and careful, but he still couldn't live without adventure. She'd known that back then, and she had accepted it. After her anger had subsided, she felt like she had been asking too much. Did she really expect Ed to change? If she was honest to herself and listened to her heart, she had to admit that she had never stopped loving him. But by the time she'd realized that, Ed was already past Mars's orbit, and she reproached herself. When contact to the spaceship was lost and NASA managers gave up on ever reestablishing it, she had been devastated. She would never be able to tell Ed how much she missed him and how much the time they had together meant to her—despite all their problems.

The driver of the SUV sat for a while in his seat with the motor off before getting out. She couldn't see him clearly behind the tinted windows, but as soon as he opened the door she recognized Jeffrey Scott, the project manager of her husband's last mission.

Scott's expression was unmoving and businesslike as he approached. She had accepted what had happened, but nevertheless a wave of grief swept over her as she realized that she was probably going to be told that her husband had officially been declared dead.

"Hello Helen. Wasn't so easy to find you."

The short man's handshake was cold and sweaty.

"The peace and quiet are good for me. There's nowhere else I want to be right now. Come in, Jeff."

"Happy to."

"Coffee?"

"Please."

Scott sat down on the couch behind the dining-room table. The house was small. There was only one room on the first floor, a living-cum-dining room with a small corner for the kitchen. A narrow wooden staircase led to two simple upstairs bedrooms. Usually, Helen sat on the small porch in the rocking chair and looked out over the wilderness. Fifty years ago, the whole property had been a farm, but the owner had given up because of the increase in droughts, and her sister had bought the place from a large property owner five years ago.

Helen put the steaming mug on the small wooden table and sat down next to the manager.

"I wasn't expecting visitors. Especially not considering the latest news."

Scott nodded. "Worse than the Cuba crisis." The atomic bomb the Chinese had dropped on the Lindbergh aircraft carrier was the latest nadir in the awful conflict. "If Moscow's negotiations fail, I don't see any hope."

"Wouldn't you rather be with your family right now?"

Scott shrugged his shoulders. "I don't have anyone I can go to. After NASA kicked me out, there's nothing left in my life that I look forward to."

"I always had the impression NASA only hires mono-maniacs."

"Possible. Our work is so complex, it doesn't leave much room for anything else. But that will change soon."

"What do you mean?"

"Haven't you heard?"

"I don't have a TV out here. And I turn off the radio when the news comes on."

"Oh. Well, NASA is being disbanded."

"Really?" Helen asked indifferently. She couldn't say she actually cared. NASA was one of the reasons her life had not been particularly happy in the past ten years.

"Yes, after the fiasco with the Helios mission, the President signed a directive closing NASA down. He'd probably just been waiting for a reason. He'd never really been a friend of civilian spaceflight. Cape Canaveral is being shut down, too. The only rockets that will still launch are military satellites from Patrick Air Force Base. JSC in Houston is also closing up shop. The Texan senator didn't even protest. MSFC in Huntsville is going to the army, and UCLA is getting JPL as a present. Half of my colleagues are out of a job. Of course none of that matters anymore if the bomb falls tomorrow. The industry also paid a price."

"The industry?"

"Centauri. You know, the multinational that cofinanced the mission. Broken up and nationalized. The entire fusion energy branch will be under the aegis of the Ministry of Energy. Antimatter technology is being split by DARPA and the army, and will only be used for weapons technology going forward. The other engine prototypes have already been scrapped." He laughed. It sounded frantic. "Two hours later, Wyman died of a heart attack. Didn't surprise me. Everything we'd worked for, all our dreams gone . . . in a matter of weeks."

"I'm sorry," said Helen, but secretly she was glad. It had been Ed's dream, not hers.

"Whatever. At any rate, expansion into space is history for America now." Scott took a sip of his coffee. "Actually, I could use something stronger."

"There's no alcohol in the house," Helen replied sternly. "Why did you come, Jeff? Not just for a cup of coffee."

"No. I came to reveal a secret to you."

"A secret?"

"A state secret. I'm not allowed to speak about it under penalty of law, but what does that matter now?"

"About Ed and his mission?"

"Yes. The public was told that after the ship suddenly disappeared, we never heard from the crew again."

"That's exactly what I was told."

"That was a lie."

Helen stared in confusion at the ex-manager.

"About thirty-two hours after last contact, the two large Deep Space Network parabolic antennas in Goldstone and Canberra both malfunctioned at the same time. Nobody knows why. No one ever found the error. When they went online again a few minutes later as suddenly as they had turned off, the end of a transmission from the Helios came through."

"Why wasn't I told?"

"Because nobody could figure it out. We assume that most of the data was lost because of the strange malfunction. The only thing that came through and could be decoded were four goodbye letters. One from each crew member."

Helen stared wide-eyed at Jeff.

"You don't mean to tell me that Ed—"

"Yes, that's what I want to tell you." He reached into his briefcase, took out a folded piece of paper, and passed it to Helen.

"From Ed? Really?"

Helen started to cry. Tears streamed down her face. Scott reached into his pocket and handed her a Kleenex.

"Why did they keep it from us? Why?"

"Right before the spaceship disappeared, the crew found something that some scientists believe is an alien artifact."

"Alien?" Helen asked skeptically.

Scott nodded. "The military were of a different opinion and were not interested in pursuing it because of the conflict with China. There's a news blackout. I had no say in it and couldn't change it. I'm sorry."

"It's OK. Thank you."

She took his hand and pressed it. Suddenly, the floor below them shook.

"What was that?" Helen asked.

"I don't know. Earthquake maybe. We should go out."

They quickly strode across the room and were standing on the porch as the shaking subsided. A low grumble as if from a faraway thunderstorm carried through the cool air. The last rays of the sun sank below the distant hills in the west.

"Oh my God," Scott whispered.

To the north, multiple thin columns of smoke rose slowly into the sky and curved toward the northeast.

"What is that?" Helen asked.

"Rockets," Scott said darkly. His voice was calm. "There must be a missile base over there. An atomic missile base, I mean. They've actually done it."

"Then the Chinese must have fired their missiles too."

"Yes, I assume so. Half an hour. At most. Do you have a cellar?"

"No."

Scott shrugged his shoulders. "Doesn't matter. Tomorrow there won't be a planet worth living on anymore anyway."

"I can't believe they've really done it. The President has children too! So do the Chinese. Our world—"

"The letter."

"What?"

"Ed's letter. If you still want to read it, this is your last chance."

She nodded. "Yes. We can sit on the porch bench."

"Sunset's over I'm afraid."

Helen looked to the west. A dark orange gave the horizon a golden tone. A blue stripe, which quickly growing darker, hung over it. A few stars were already twinkling in the sky.

"At least we can see the night sky one last time. Since I got here, I often sit outside at night and stargaze in the clear air. Often I think the stars are the last bit of nature we humans haven't destroyed. Maybe it's good that we'll never reach them."

"The letter!"

Helen nodded. "Yes."

Her hands shaking, she unfolded the letter. It had four paragraphs. She began reading slowly.

Dearest Helen …

"Who's that?" Scott asked.

Helen looked over to where Scott was staring. There was a man standing under the trees near the well, looking at them.

Helen stood up. She couldn't make out the man's face in the twilight. He raised his hand in greeting and stepped forward. Helen still couldn't see his features, but she knew who it was immediately from the gesture.

She felt dizzy and put out a hand to steady herself. The letter fluttered to the floor. Then Ed reached the light and Scott gasped.

"Well I'll be damned!" the NASA manager said.

Ed strode slowly across the dusty yard to the front steps of the porch.

"Ed!" Helen didn't know what was going on. For a second, she thought she was dreaming. Maybe the missiles had hit and she'd died without noticing it? No, that was ridiculous. But how could …?

"Ed!" She went slowly down the stairs until she was right in front of him, his face looking down at hers. She felt his warmth, smelled the scent she knew so well, and was sure she wasn't dreaming.

"What's going on? How can you possibly be here?" Scott groaned.

"Is it really you?" Helen asked.

Ed nodded. "It's really me," he answered, reaching for

her hands. Her touch hit him like an electric shock. Whatever she wanted to say to him, she better do it fast.

"The atomic missiles ..." she said.

Ed shook his head. "... won't reach their target."

It sounded too good to be true. Just like his unexpected return. Which is why she knew he was telling the truth.

"Then you'll stay here?" she asked.

Ed nodded. "Yes. I'll stay here, with you."

For a long moment, they looked each other silently in the eyes. Then he leaned forward to kiss her.

Afterword

For years now, experiments with quantum teleportation have been conducted, albeit only with photons and atoms. Anton Zeilinger's *Dance of the Photons: From Einstein to Quantum Teleportation* provides a good introduction to the topic.

Warp drive as described in this book was first postulated by Miguel Alcubierre in 1994. Since then, many physicists have worked theoretically on the principle of faster-than-light travel. However it is highly doubtful that it will ever be put into practice. Many scientific papers explore this principle, as well as *Frontiers of Propulsion Science* by Marc G. Mills et al.

Nobody knows the exact geometry of the universe. Most cosmological theories assume the universe is either infinite or a hypersphere. But more exotic geometries are certainly possible. One book that looks at these possibilities explicitly is *The Wraparound Universe* by the French physicist Jean-Pierre Luminet. Max Tegmark's visionary book *Our Mathematical Universe*, which deals with infinite inflation and various concepts of parallel worlds, is also well worth reading.

The man who first proposed the idea of cosmic inflation, Alan Guth, has also written a book that anyone interested in the topic should read, aptly entitled *The Inflationary Universe*. Those interested in different models of universes should not miss *The Book of Universes* by John D. Barrow.

Dark Flow was first observed in 2008 during systematic analyses of WMAP satellite data. To this day, the discussion rages on whether these observations were correct or a misinterpretation. One article on the topic is: "A measurement of large-scale peculiar velocities of clusters of galaxies: results and cosmological implications" by A. Kashlinsky et al. (*Astrophys. J.*686:L49-L52, 2009)

Neither space-time defects nor domain borders are figments of my imagination, but have been discussed in numerous cosmological papers and books, for example: Tanmay Vachaspati, *Kinks and Domain Walls—An Introduction to Classical and Quantum Solitons* (Cambridge: Cambridge University Press, 2006).

Others before me have also discussed using wormholes for time travel. Richard Gott provides a good theoretical overview in his *Time Travel in Einstein's Universe*.

There are many biographies of Albert Einstein himself. The best, in my opinion, is *Einstein—His Life and Universe* by Walter Isaacson.

Paradox 2 – Beyond Eternity

March 2018

First published in German as

Paradox 2—Jenseits der Ewigkeit

November 2017

Author:

Phillip P. Peterson

Publisher:

Peter Bourauel

Auelswiese 2

53783 Eitorf

raumvektor@gmx.de

German editors:

Anke Höhl-Kayser

Andrea Weil

Translator:

Laura Radosh

English editor:

Jenny Piening

Cover:

Buzzart/99designs

✿ Created with Vellum

82937686R00149

Made in the USA
Middletown, DE
07 August 2018